"I'm starting to see that you weren't pretending... unless you are now?"

Sean wasn't sure how to respond to that. With Paisley in his arms, he couldn't think straight. He was doing his best not to kiss her, to claim the kiss that he'd been craving since he'd walked away from her that night everything went wrong.

But he also didn't want to gloss over this moment. He could count on one hand the times that someone had simply hugged him and made him feel cared for the way that Paisley was doing right now.

"I'm not faking it, Paisley. Though I have no idea what I'm doing and I'm sort of winging it."

She smiled. "Me too. I want...I want this Christmas to be a new start for us. What do you say?"

"I'd like that too. No more secrets."

* * *

Billionaire Fake Out by Katherine Garbera
is part of the The Image Project series.

Dear Reader,

I can't believe the last book in The Image Project is here. I had the best time writing this series and hope you enjoyed reading it.

One of the things I love exploring is how relationships change over time and how something said to a stranger can have a deeper impact when they are no longer one. That's part of what's going on in this story with Sean/Jack. Paisley was just a hot girl in line in front of him at a coffee shop, they flirted, hooked up and then without him meaning for it to happen, he sort of started a relationship with her. One that was rooted in the lie he told her when she was a stranger.

Paisley has always been the mother hen of the IDG Brand Imaging women and takes care of everyone else because of her past. But she prides herself on having a keen eye for BS and isn't sure how Sean slipped past that.

I really enjoyed writing this book and this series. This book takes place during the Christmas season, which is one of my favorite times of the year.

Happy reading!

Katherine

KATHERINE GARBERA

BILLIONAIRE FAKE OUT

Recycling programs for this product may not exist in your area.

ISBN-13: 978-1-335-58166-2

Billionaire Fake Out

Copyright © 2023 by Katherine Garbera

For questions and comments about the quality of this book, please contact us at CustomerService@Harlequin.com.

Harlequin Enterprises ULC
22 Adelaide St. West, 41st Floor
Toronto, Ontario M5H 4E3, Canada
www.Harlequin.com

Printed in U.S.A.

Katherine Garbera is the *USA TODAY* bestselling author of more than a hundred and twenty-five novels. She's a small-town Florida girl whose imagination was fired up by long hours spent outside sitting underneath orange trees. She grew up to travel the world and makes her home in the UK with her husband. Her books have garnered numerous awards and are sold around the world. Connect with her at www.katherinegarbera.com and on Facebook, Instagram and Twitter.

Books by Katherine Garbera

Harlequin Desire

Destination Wedding

The Wedding Dare
The One from the Wedding
Secrets of a Wedding Crasher

The Image Project

Billionaire Makeover
The Billionaire Plan
Billionaire Fake Out

Visit the Author Profile page
at Harlequin.com for more titles.

You can also find Katherine Garbera on Facebook, along with other Harlequin Desire authors, at Facebook.com/HarlequinDesireAuthors!

This one is dedicated, as many of them are, to my family. I was lucky to be born into a family of loving, supportive parents and to have two wonderful sisters to share my crazy upbringing with. I was also extremely lucky to have two children who changed my world and made me grow in ways I didn't realize I could. I am lucky to have found love with a man who shared a few of my bumps and bruises, and helped me to make them into strengths and who brought into our family four amazing stepchildren. Our adult children have found really good partners who get them and bring out their strengths. We are blessed with two lovely granddaughters.

So to Charlotte, David, Donna, Linda, Rob, Courtney, Lucas, Georgina, Bobby, Brooke, Penny, Josh, Darcey, Tabitha, Wendy and Bella—this one is for you with love.

One

Pregnant.

She shook her head, staring down at the over-the-counter pregnancy test she'd taken. *Again.* She had to be reading the results wrong.

Please let her be reading it wrong.

Paisley Campbell wasn't having the best day. Her brother had called to say that their elderly dog, Pasha, was being taken to the vet because of another stroke, while one of her clients was sure that if he just went on TV and earnestly protested he was being unfairly treated for calling the cops on the homeless man who'd been scrounging through his dumpster the public would "get it," and the fifth pregnancy test she'd taken in as many days still read positive.

All three areas of her normally neatly ordered life were in chaos. But right now, the pregnancy bombshell was at the forefront of her mind.

How had she let this happen?

It wasn't that she was a rigid rule follower, though she also wasn't really impulsive, either. And it would be so easy to blame Jack and his big, sexy brown eyes that made her forget everything, even her own name. But the truth was there was something solid about the man that made her feel safe, like she'd found a home with him in a way that nothing and no one had since her parents' divorce.

Not smart, but then Paisley knew that emotions seldom times were. She had to tell him about the pregnancy. There was no use putting it off after the five tests. She could rule it a fluke after one or two, but not five. Also, he had texted her earlier, telling her to put on her best dress and meet him at one of the fanciest restaurants in the Chicagoland area because he had big news.

She wasn't sure what he had up his sleeve. Maybe he'd finally gotten a decent job. Which she knew sounded judgy, but he'd been working at the gym around the corner from her place for the last six months, and frankly, it wasn't like he was a world-class trainer. Or maybe he was, she thought. She really had no idea what it was he did there.

But he didn't bring home the big bucks. That, she knew for sure. Jack had been living with her since their second date. He did cook and pay for all of their meals, but otherwise he didn't contribute to their living expenses other than sometimes putting hundred-dollar bills in her wallet. Which was odd, but she didn't mind.

It wasn't his wallet that had caught her eye; it was his ass in those tight jeans he'd been wearing. And besides, she could afford her lifestyle. She was hungry to grow the business she and her friends co-owned, IDG Brand Imaging. They were big in the Midwest but she wanted to take them national. She knew there were bigger, well-established companies in California and New York, but she was eyeing them and planning to go bigger soon.

Paisley finished applying her lipstick and then checked her hair. She'd put it up in a low chignon. She had full bangs that covered her forehead and, she thought, framed her facial features in a flattering way. The dress she wore was a cream-colored velvet sheath with an organza overdress with flowers embroidered over it. It hugged her body, and as she turned to catch her side view, she realized it wouldn't fit her for much longer.

The baby.

She'd managed to do a nice job of not really facing the fact that she was pregnant. She looked at herself in the mirror. She had always wanted to have a family…someday. The truth was this little bun in the oven didn't feel real to her. Probably wouldn't until she saw how Jack reacted. And honestly, she had no idea what his reaction would be.

Paisley was sort of afraid and she hadn't allowed herself to be afraid in a really long time. She was good at finding the bright side of things, but this… was bigger than her. She wanted to text Olive and Delaney because she needed her best friends by her side at a time like this.

But it was Jack's baby and she sort of thought he should be the first one she told. Plus, they had this date tonight. She hoped… She took a deep breath. In her head she was picturing his reaction and it was, of course, something over-the-top in the best possible way. But so many times life didn't deliver on her expectations.

"Stop!" she told herself. Sometimes her mind kept going on and on and nothing she could say would put a kibosh on it.

She put on her red velvet cloak, because it was December in Chicago, but she also liked to look festive during the holiday season. Then, taking a bolstering breath, she walked out of her building and saw that Delaney's Rolls-Royce was waiting at the curb.

"Good evening, Ms. Campbell. I'm at your service tonight," her friend's driver, Lyle, said as he stepped out of the car.

"Do you know where we are going?"

"Yes, ma'am. All you have to do is sit and relax," he assured her.

Lyle opened the back door to the Rolls and she saw a gaily wrapped present on the seat and an envelope with her name on it.

As soon as she was settled in and had her seat belt on, she opened the envelope. There was some really nice thick paper folded in half and a note from Jack. She'd recognize his heavy, scrawly handwriting anywhere.

> Paisley,
> Tonight I want you to forget about the real world and let me sweep you away. It's my way of saying thank you for the last six months.
> Jack

Her heart leaped to her throat. Did that mean he wanted to go beyond six months? Or was he saying goodbye in the nicest way possible?

Paisley stepped out of the silver Rolls-Royce and Sean caught his breath as he always did when he saw her. She had pretty blue-gray eyes in a heart-shaped face with the thick fall of brown bangs on her forehead and always looked beautiful.

But tonight she was positively *radiant*.

Her dress was a true showstopper. It had a high, elegant neckline and slighty puffed, black lace sleeves that had been embroidered with stars and a swirling moon similar to van Gogh's famous painting *The Starry Night*. The dress itself was a fit-and-flare type that hugged her arms and breasts, and showed off her slim waist before falling in a cascade of what looked like velvet from this distance. The designer had continued the stars-and-moon embroidery on the skirt and it ended at her ankles. He saw the pointed toes of her cream-colored leather stiletto-heeled boots peeking out from under the hem. And she held a vintage Chanel quilted chain bag in her hands.

Yet despite her poise and grace, the way she was standing there staring at him, she looked almost… nervous. Like maybe, despite the skullcap he had on, she could tell he'd changed his hair back to its normal color. Maybe she'd figured out who he was.

Or maybe not.

Regardless, tonight he was going to come clean about his real identity. But he didn't want to do it in her apartment, which he'd been sharing with her for the last six months. He wanted the reveal of his true self to show all the parts he'd been hiding.

To that end, he'd pulled out all the stops. He had booked out the entire restaurant, dyed his hair back to its natural dark brown and shaved off the beard he'd been sporting since they'd first met. And as for his attire? He'd donned his signature designer Hugo Boss suit. He had an ad campaign with them that had launched over the Thanksgiving weekend, and ironically, he'd spotted the billboard on his way here tonight.

She smiled at him and he smiled right back at her as his eyes once again drank in the gorgeous woman standing before him. She had the fur muff that he'd given to her as a gift in her hands, and the long red velvet opera cloak that she loved to wear was over one arm.

When she noticed the horse-drawn coach behind him, she nodded.

"At first I was like, what the heck, now it makes sense," she said as she walked toward him. When she got closer, he noticed that some snowflakes were stuck to her hair and he reached up to brush them off as he took her cloak and wrapped it around her shoulders.

"Is it too cold for this?" he asked, gesturing to the horse and carriage.

"No way! I love this," she gushed. "You look good in all black and clean-shaven. Almost like someone else I know… How did I never notice what a strong jawline you have?"

"Because you're usually eyeing other parts of my body," he said with a wink.

"That's hardly my fault—you have a very fine ass."

Sean laughed and helped her into the carriage, covering their legs with the thick wool blanket as soon as he joined her. The carriage driver handed them a thermos with hot chocolate in it, then turned and they were off.

He took a deep breath as he slid his arm around her slender shoulders and pulled her into the curve of his body. For a moment, he knew if he just kept being Jack, nothing had to change. He could let go of his nerves and continue playing this part.

But for how long?

He couldn't lie to her forever and he had to be back in LA at the end of the week to start doing press. He had to tell her tonight. There were no more excuses that even he could accept.

Sean wanted to be the romantic leading man that he'd played a time or two. He wanted Paisley to feel like she was the center of the universe and that his lie hadn't been perpetrated to hurt her, but had been played out in order to protect her.

He rubbed the back of his neck, wondering how his practical and frank girlfriend was going to react to that admission. The hard part was that he knew he should have said something sooner.

Like two weeks ago, when she'd invited him to spend Christmas with her. As she'd been lying in his arms in front of the electric glow of her plug-in fireplace, he'd felt closer to contentment than he'd ever felt before.

He had almost let the truth slip then, but didn't. Until filming wrapped, he didn't like to talk about his characters. And in truth, the man he'd been playing was very close to his Chicago persona, Jack. He could play up the fact that there were blurred lines. But the trust was more complicated and he prayed that Paisley would see that too, if she even talked to him after this evening.

"Your note was a bit cryptic," she said.

"Was it?" he asked. "It was meant to be romantic."

"I can see that now. But I wasn't sure if you meant

it as a big thank-you for six months of sex as you headed out the door or not."

He winced. Had he given that vibe intentionally? Because he knew that once he told her who he was, everything would change. It didn't matter that Paisley was different from the rest of the world. She understood celebrity and public image better than most. But it didn't mean she was going to give him a free pass for not fessing up sooner.

"Glad you can see that now," he said. "But I do have something big I want to share with you."

"Good—me too," she admitted.

She had big news? He had been so focused on this huge reveal he hadn't really been paying as much attention to Paisley as he would have liked. Granted, he knew this thing between them wasn't love; he just didn't have that inside of him. Sean hadn't grown up in a nurturing, loving home. And, as a result, he'd gotten good at *acting* like he was in love, but the truth was he was pretty sure he'd never felt it. But he liked her. And he wanted to keep seeing her after he returned to his life in LA.

"Ladies first," he said.

He told himself that was the gentlemanly thing to do. After all, he knew she'd been working harder than ever in the last few weeks, trying to land some clients outside of the Midwest. He'd listened to her plans for the future many nights while they'd been lying together in bed. He liked the way she dreamed and shared it with him.

It was so different from the women he'd known in LA. They were always telling him how he could help them get to where they wanted to be. But Paisley wasn't looking for a shortcut.

"No, that's okay. I want to hear your news," she said at last, taking one of her hands out of the muff and putting it on his gloved one. Her fingers were delicate, and the way she looked up at him was so open and a little bit vulnerable.

He told himself he had nothing to feel guilty about, but that didn't stop him from feeling it. Also, it seemed like something about her was a little bit off and he wondered once again if she'd somehow already learned his identity. That would make this easier.

"Does your news concern me?" he asked her. If she said yes, he'd just go into his prepared speech about confidentiality on the set and all that.

"It does," she whispered. "But I know I'm going to make a mess of telling you. So I just need a few more minutes to gather my thoughts."

"Come here," he said, pulling her into his arms and kissing her. His intention had been to comfort her, but then his best-laid plans went south as passion flared inside him. Her mouth was hard to resist when he knew he'd never be able to kiss her again. And now, with the uncertainty of her reaction to the truth, he needed her even more.

She wrapped her arms around his shoulders and

kissed him back, tipping her head to the side as he deepened the lip-lock. God, how he wanted her.

He lifted his head. "Did that help soothe your nerves?"

Instead of answering, she averted her gaze.

Her reaction didn't sit well with him. What was it she had to tell him that was making her this anxious? But right now, he had to reveal *his* news.

"Uh, well, this isn't going to be easy—"

Her eyes darted back to his. "You said you weren't saying goodbye," she interrupted.

"I'm not."

"Then what is it?" she asked.

"I'm not who you think I am. I mean, I am but I'm also more." For the love of all that was holy, how the hell had he ever won an Oscar with this kind of rambling nonsense. He wished he had called one of his screenwriter buddies and gotten him to script the scene for him.

She furrowed her brow. "What are you saying, Jack?"

"I haven't been totally honest with you about my job situation," he said at last.

"I figured," she replied with a wry look. Her eyebrows arched and she gave him what he thought of as her I-mean-business face. "Granted, I don't know what kind of occupation you have, but that gym you have me drop you off at doesn't look like it's very successful—" Her eyes widened. "Wait, do you do something illegal?" she asked.

"No! Listen, there's no easy way to say this," he began as the carriage made the turn to take them back to the restaurant. Out of the corner of his eye, he thought he caught some movement in the bushes, but he didn't want to be distracted from Paisley, who was looking up at him in anticipation.

"I'm not Jack Nelson, as I told you. I'm really—"

"Sean O'Neill, over here!"

"Fuck," he muttered.

She looked around in confusion, trying to find Sean O'Neill, and then her gaze went back to Jack. As she continued looking at him, he saw the moment when realization dawned.

"Have you been hiding out in Chicago because your ex just got remarried to space-tech billionaire Ainsley Hartman?" a paparazzo asked as flashbulbs went off around them.

Jack brought up his hand and pulled up the blanket from their lap in order to cover their faces. In the intimate cocoon under it, he turned to face Paisley.

"Ex-wife?" Paisley gasped. Then she sat back and glared at him before reaching over to pull the beanie off his head. "Sean O'Neill!"

Two

Paisley almost couldn't process everything he'd said. Of course, the paparazzi's flashbulbs and a million questions being screamed at them didn't help. The driver of the carriage thankfully picked up the pace and by the time they were back at the restaurant, several security guards awaited them. She couldn't even look at Jack—*Sean*.

Her mind was spinning with so many questions she felt dizzy. One…was he married? And, two, had she really been dating a Hollywood A-lister? She wasn't sure about the married thing, but the part about him being a famous celebrity was undeniable. In fact, the man was so damn famous that she felt stupid for not having recognized him.

To be fair, he'd definitely altered his looks by dyeing his hair blond and wearing the beard and mustache. But at the same time, how had she missed that? It made her realize how much she'd made Jack into the man she wanted him to be and not really seen him for who he actually was. Yet, now that she knew he was Sean O'Neill, it was impossible not to see. "Have you been wearing colored contacts?"

"Uh, yes."

And what did it say about her that she almost wished he'd been a criminal. Somehow that would have been easier to handle than this.

Anything would be easier than this.

But why was she surprised? When had life ever been as smooth and easy as the last six months with Jack—*Sean!*—had been?

The doorman offered her his hand and she climbed down, almost slipping on the icy pavement. And as she felt herself slipping, she put her hand on her stomach. The baby. Her baby with— Not now. She couldn't. Paisley steadied herself, felt Sean's hand on her back and deliberately stepped away from him and inside the lobby of the restaurant. She scanned it until she saw the women's bathroom and made a beeline for it, dropping the fur muff he'd given to her on the floor as she went.

She wanted nothing from him. Not ever again, she thought as tears started to burn in her eyes and her breaths came too fast. She stopped immediately inside the ladies' room as the door shut behind her.

Then, leaning against the tiled wall, she closed her eyes and began doing some breathing techniques that her therapist had taught her, during her parents' divorce.

Breathe in and count of four. Hold it.

But how could she hold it when the man who had fathered her baby was an imposter. He wasn't anything like the man—

Stop. Just breathe.

She fumbled in the pocket of her cloak for her phone and pulled it out, then placed a video call to Delaney and Olive. She needed her friends. They'd ground her and make this all okay. They'd give her some sage advice or maybe even make her laugh.

Olive answered first and a moment later Delaney did as well.

"What's wrong?" Olive immediately asked.

"OMG. You look horrible! What happened?" Delaney cried. "Do you need us? Lyle just got back."

"I can't… Jack isn't who he said he was. He's really the actor Sean O'Neill."

"Bastard," Delaney hissed.

"Uh, Pais, are you sure about this?" Olive asked. "Sean O'Neill is known for his piercing blue eyes… Jack has brown ones."

"He wore color contacts and dyed his hair. He was totally lying to me the entire time," Paisley said, feeling real panic set in.

"F— I'm googling the details," Olive said.

"I'm on my way," Delaney added.

"Can you pick me up, Dellie?" Olive asked.

"Yes. On my way."

"Pais, what do you need?"

"I don't know. I thought… Girls, I'm pregnant. I was going to tell him tonight but now, how can I? I don't know this man. Everything he's ever said is a lie. I'm mortified that I didn't realize."

"Pregnant? Okay," Olive said. "Are we happy about it?"

"I was. I don't know," Paisley choked out.

"Fuck him," Delaney said. "You're going to be a wonderful mom. Don't let him steal this from you."

"Thanks, girls."

"Of course," they both said at once.

The emotions were overwhelming her and she was starting to cry. She couldn't believe she'd been so *stupid* about him. About this entire thing. She wanted to get out of here and never see him again.

But how?

The paparazzi were probably still out there. He might be too. She had to make a plan.

"Actually, on second thought, don't come here. Let me get out of the restaurant first and then…"

"You have no car," Delaney pointed out. "If I show up, I can distract the photographers."

She shook her head. She couldn't let her friends solve this for her. "I will take care of this. I just… I was so shook I needed to talk."

"Believe me, we get that, Pais," Delaney said. "I'm going to send Lyle to come get you. You don't need to wait for an Uber. He'll text you when he's there. Come out when you are ready."

"And I'm going to send you all the info I can find on Sean and his life. Call us when you are home," Olive told her.

"I will. Thank you both."

"We love you," Delaney said.

"I love you both too."

She hung up, wiped the tears off her face and turned to face herself in the mirror. She'd been lied to before. Her dad had done it for years. But she knew she'd find a way to get through this. She had no choice, really, because she still had the baby to think about...

Paisley splashed water on her face and as the water went down the drain, she tried to tell herself all her belief and affection for Ja— For Sean did too. But it wasn't that easy. She'd was still in a state of shock.

However, right now, she needed to switch to survival mode because she was going to have to face him before she left. She sighed. Well, fortunately for her, survival mode was what she did best. Having grown up the daughter of a con man, she and her family had moved around a lot when one of his schemes was either found out, or he'd run out of marks. The reason for their relocating was something that Paisley hadn't realized until she was in college. She had mistakenly believed her father was being transferred around because of his work.

God, she was an idiot when it came to men. She'd believed her father all those years and had convinced herself she had a good bullshit meter, but now…she was questioning that.

How had she let Sean O'Neill fool her? He was one of the most lauded actors of their generation, but still, she'd always believed she was smarter than that.

She needed to get her head in the right space. She looked at herself in the mirror.

"You're a badass," she told her reflection. "You deserve to be loved by someone who doesn't lie to you. And that man doesn't deserve to see your pain."

Then she straightened her shoulders and prayed that somehow she could get through the next hour without completely breaking down. She just wanted to get out of this restaurant and back—

Dammit.

He'd been living in the home she'd made for herself. She'd invited this liar into her sanctuary. But she'd worry about that later. Right now she had to get out of here.

Stay strong, Paisley. She took a deep, bracing breath, turned toward the door and opened it.

That could have gone better.

Sean was standing in the lobby area of the restaurant. The security guards were taking care of the paparazzi. But that was the least of his problems. He saw the muff that had been a gift on the floor, picked it up and realized how fucked up this all was. Anger rolled through him as he balled his fists, wanting to punch something. He took a few breaths to try to calm down, but when he screwed up this big, it wasn't easy.

He wished there was a way he could push the blame for this onto the photographers and gossip sites that had been waiting for them, but he knew *he* was responsible for this entire mess.

Trouble was, he just wasn't sure how to fix it. His mind was running through a lifetime of acting roles, trying to find the right words and emotions to remedy this situation, but he came up empty. After all, he'd never played a man who had lied to a woman like Paisley.

That was a big part of the problem here. She wasn't like anything he'd ever experienced before. Of course, with his inflated ego and his expectation that he could get anyone to forgive him, he'd just done what he needed to do for the role, never realizing how deeply he could hurt her. Or that, unlike in the past, he wasn't going to be able to charm his way out of this. Most people allowed him more grace than he knew he deserved. But Paisley wasn't *most people*. He'd known that, but had allowed his arrogance to convince him he could smooth things over, anyway.

At first he'd told himself it was just sex that was drawing them together, but as the months went by he'd started to realize it was more than their hot physical attraction that kept him coming back for more. He genuinely liked Paisley and hadn't meant to cause her any pain. But he couldn't afford any press leaks, and as much as he cared for the beautiful brand-imaging expert, he hadn't been able to trust her with the truth.

He realized now that she wasn't going to accept that excuse.

He wished…well, that he felt something other than guilt, anger and regret. He knew he should feel more, but that emptiness inside of him just echoed like the cavern it was. He couldn't even fake it around her because this was Paisley and he wanted to be real.

But when had he ever been?

He heard the door to the ladies' room open and glanced over to see her emerge. Her eyes were red, the disgust and outrage clear on her face.

"I'm sorry." That always seemed a good place to start.

She just nodded her head stiffly.

"I want to get past this."

"I don't see that happening," she told him.

"So you're just going to stay mad at me?"

"Yes."

"That's completely justified," he said.

"Why did you lie to me?"

"I signed an NDA before coming out here to work and the press is insane. That little thing with the paparazzi was just a taster. Normally they hound me everywhere—"

"I get it. You're super famous and everyone wants

something from you. But I didn't. I just thought you were this sweet, hot guy."

Those words… Was this more than regret and guilt sweeping through him? He wasn't sure. All he knew for certain was that this woman *mattered*. He reached for her and this time he allowed his hand to fall on her shoulder.

Maybe there was a chance to save this. She wasn't pushing him away physically.

But as he leaned in to kiss her, she turned her head away.

"Okay…" He cleared his throat. "Do you want dinner?"

"Are you kidding me right now?" she snapped, and he saw her mask slip as anger flashed. "I am barely keeping everything in check. So, no, I can't pretend everything is okay and dine with you."

"Understood." He put his hands up. "What can I do?"

"Don't talk to me. I'm waiting for Lyle to come back and then I'm going home. You can come and get your stuff tomorrow."

He was starting to get the feeling that she was cutting him out of her life. That felt…like something he hadn't felt since he'd been legally emancipated from his mom when he was seventeen. Suck it up, he told himself. He had always known there would be consequences for deceiving her.

But he had traded on their closeness. He thought

the bond they'd created as lovers would be something that could bridge this. How had he read her wrong?

"Okay."

"Is that all you're going to say to me?"

He scrubbed a hand over his face then released a ragged breath. "Let's be honest, Paisley. There isn't anything I can say at this moment that you will actually hear. I mean, even a screenwriter—"

"Don't do that. Be the man you truly are. I don't want you to act a part...but that's what you've been doing since the moment we met, isn't it?"

Jack, his alter ego, would lie and soothe her, but she wanted the real man. "Yes, it is. I mean, at first you were just this sexy woman with a cute smile and I didn't know you so I wasn't intentionally lying."

"But once you knew me? You lived in my apartment, Sean. You should have said something. I let you into my life..."

"I know," he said quietly.

"Why now?" she asked. "I mean, the lie was going so well for you."

He rubbed the back of his neck. If he had actual emotions, he thought, that jab of hers would have hurt. "I'm done filming and heading back to LA on Monday."

"Oh."

He'd never in his life heard her sound so small and almost...broken.

"I was hoping we could figure out a way to keep seeing each other," he said.

"Were you? Why?"

"I like you," he admitted. That was the God's honest truth.

"I don't like you."

"That's your anger talking, and I'm not saying you aren't justified. But we both know that you like me too."

"I don't like Sean O'Neill. I liked *Jack* but he was someone you made up and probably also someone I created. Not real. I don't know Sean O'Neill…" She trailed off, her voice cracking, and her hands started to shake as she wrapped her arms around her waist.

He didn't know if she could ever forgive him. And honestly, he wasn't sure that he deserved it. All the months that he'd been telling himself he could make this right, he'd been lying to himself.

She needed more than a guy who was playing a role. More than someone who was following a script and using it as a guide to be a man who was worthy of her. And Sean realized he might not ever be that person.

Hell, chances were he wasn't. But he couldn't just leave her. He knew that was what she wanted but it wasn't something he was prepared to do right now.

"Can we start over?" he asked gruffly.

"No, we can't."

A muscle ticked in his jaw. "Why not? I'm not entirely a monster," he said.

"But you are *partially*?"

"Well, I'm pretty sure you think I am."

"Not a monster. Just a stranger," she said.

"Then let's fix it. In retrospect, I wish I'd told you sooner, but I was doing some research for the role and starting filming, and I didn't know you."

He reached for her again, and this time she relaxed for a moment, letting him draw her closer. But as he leaned down to kiss her, he saw her eyes widen and there was sheen of tears there. She shook her head and pulled back again.

Something ached inside of him as she withdrew, but he let her go, stepping aside to give her some space.

"I get it. I mean, I run a PR and brand-management company. I make my living from using the press and leaking things."

Somehow, hearing it from her mouth sounded worse than it had in his head. He heard it as the excuse it was. All of that might have been true for the first few weeks, but once he'd gotten to know Paisley…he knew she'd never betray a trust.

He'd just never really liked himself or who he was when he wasn't playing a role. He'd grown up in front of the camera and he knew that it was an excuse he used to justify all his shortcomings, but at the same time, it was the truth.

"I'm sorry."

"I know, and I wish I could forgive you, but I can't."

"And you can't start over, either. So what's next?" he asked.

She took a deep breath and let it out in one long exhalation. "I honestly don't know."

The way he kept staring at her made Paisley realize that the gifted actor known for his emotional depth was looking at her with vacant eyes that revealed nothing.

His skin had gone kind of ashen, so she knew he must be feeling something. But what? And this was new. In the past she'd have rushed to Jack's side to reassure him, but this wasn't Jack. This was Sean. And Sean was a stranger. One who was used to playing to the crowd, and in this room, there was only the two of them.

"No forgiveness? That's not really like you, Pais," he said, gritting out the words.

"Call me 'Ms. Campbell,' Mr. O'Neill. After all, we don't really know each other," she said, wishing she could sit down. Anger was still there, a quiet little ember deep inside of her. But they did have things to discuss. And it might be better to have this conversation in private. But where? Her place? She couldn't bear the thought of having him back there.

"We need to talk," he said. "I have a hotel—"

"You what?"

"I have a hotel suite here in town," he said. "I use it for working and meetings and that sort of thing. We can go there and talk."

"Fine."

But in her mind, she added another lie to the list.

This was worse than she'd realized. He had been living an entire life away from her and she'd never cottoned on to it. She knew her friends would say it was because she saved her trust for those people who earned it. How had she let Sean earn it when he'd been lying? Probably his hotter-than-summer kisses and that rock-hard body of his. Something that obviously had bitten her in the ass.

"I'm sorry."

"I know. You said it a few times already." She lifted her chin. "These lies may have been orchestrated to protect your privacy, but I never saw any of the signs. So I'm standing here feeling dumber and dumber with each knew revelation. And I'm just one lie away from totally losing it."

He stepped forward, put his hands on her shoulders and looked her square in the eye. "I understand. But please believe me when I say I'm not hiding anything else. And from this moment forward, I won't lie to you, even if it would serve me better to keep quiet. Ask me anything."

She wanted to believe him as a shiver of sensual awareness went through her. Did that make her the most pitiful woman alive? She hoped not. But honestly, it didn't matter if it did. She needed to believe him. Sean was the father of her unborn child. He was a stranger and yet his face was so endearingly familiar. He'd been a man she'd thought she was falling for.

Now she wasn't as sure. She wanted answers and

she was going to have to take him at his word, or send him on his way. Those were her two options.

Could she keep him around her if she didn't trust him? And how long was it going to take for her to trust him again…if ever?

She stepped back, forcing him to release his grip on her. "Were you living in the hotel when we met?"

"Yes, I was."

"Then why did you move in with me?" she asked.

"You asked," he said simply.

"If I hadn't?"

"I would have kept seeing you but stayed at the hotel at night," he replied. "But I like your place and I really got a chance to see the real Paisley there. Not just that cute girl who smiled at me in the coffee line. I liked the quirky way you look at the world and how you created a home for us."

"But *did* you? I mean you weren't really Jack. And that home was mine, not ours," she said.

His jaw tightened. "You are completely justified to keep taking jabs at me, but I am only human. I made a mistake and I've apologized."

She sighed.

He was right. "Fine. I'll try to be fair. But it's hard because while I know we need to talk, I'm still really pissed at you and at myself. I feel stupid, Sean. You're really famous. Even with the disguise and the colored contacts, I should have recognized you."

"You're not stupid. You didn't see it because you have a good heart and believed I was who I said."

A good heart.

Sean couldn't know that her father had once said the exact same thing to her. His praise had been something that he'd used to manipulate her. Was that what Sean was doing? She swallowed. But the man standing before her wasn't her father. This situation wasn't the same. He wasn't asking her to hide something from the rest of her family.

"I'll try to hold my tongue," she said as her phone pinged. She glanced down to see that Delaney's driver had arrived. "Lyle is here. He can take us to your hotel."

He gestured for her to lead the way and they stepped outside into the inky December darkness. She moved cautiously, not wanting to slip again. Lyle waited by the car, holding open the door for her. He quirked one eyebrow as he noticed Sean behind her.

"Will you be accompanied?"

"I will. We are going to a hotel that Mr. O'Neill will give you the address for."

She got into the back seat of the car, slid over and looked out the window, realizing that the snow from earlier had turned to a slushy rain.

Fitting.

She'd seen only the fairy-tale ending she'd wanted for herself, but now that she'd shaken off the pixie dust, she took in the real world around her. Not the beginning of something special, but just another cold, dark winter night.

Sean got into the car beside her and Lyle closed

the door firmly. Sean looked as if he was going to talk to her and she turned her body so she could stare out the window. How could she still want him after all he'd done to her? But she did. She wanted to crawl across the seat, climb on his lap and kiss him until she forgot the truth he'd dropped on her tonight. Wrong or right, she wanted to use his body and somehow convince herself that she had really known the man whose baby she was having.

But she didn't. As much as her body craved his, she thought as she stared out the window at the passing scenery, she knew that wasn't a solution.

She was alone in the world and always had been. It was something she wished she'd remembered before she let him into her life.

Three

The snow had turned to a wintery mix of rain and sleet, which wasn't at all romantic or sexy, and he felt like whoever was directing this moment had gotten the setting right. But this wasn't a film. No one was going to call "cut" and there was no chance he was going to be able to "explain" things to Paisley and tell her it was just a scene.

This was *life*.

The one thing he always struggled to make right. So here he was, staring at her profile and trying to find words that would make her look at him. Make her laugh. He wanted to see her smile. It was truly one of the most beautiful things about her, and in his gut, he felt like he wasn't going to get to see it again.

"So…"

Yeah, he was eloquent. Not.

She turned to face him and he noticed the glimmer of tears in her eyes—he felt like the bastard he'd been told he could be. No matter what his intentions had been, he'd done something unpardonable. And for once the man with the plan had no idea what to do next.

"I can't do this tonight. I thought I could, but I need time," she said softly. Leaning forward, she tapped Lyle on the shoulder. "Could you take me home first and then take Mr. O'Neill to his hotel?"

Without turning his head or taking his gaze from the road, Lyle changed lanes. "Of course, ma'am."

She sat back and crossed her hands in her lap. He noticed how calm she tried to be but he sensed… well, it didn't take a genius to figure out she was barely holding herself together. But she still looked so gorgeous and sexy. It was all he could do to keep his hands to himself. He knew that the last thing she wanted right now was to be in his arms, yet that was what he wanted. He felt if he held her again, they could figure this out.

"What can I do?" he asked. At this point, all he really could offer was whatever she needed.

"Just leave me alone," she said.

Her words were well deserved, but they still stung. He had to fix things with Paisley but he had no idea how. "I want to help make this right."

She gave him a look that would have broken a weaker man.

"I can't do this right now," she reiterated. "Give me some space and we can talk later."

He raked a hand through his hair and nodded. "Yes, of course, we can. I just want you to know that I never meant to hurt you."

She shook her head. "Great. I've got a man with good intentions who lied to me at my side."

Then she dropped her head and looked at her clenched hands. "I'm sorry. I know you apologized but I didn't expect you to lie. How did I not see the signs?"

He knew it was a rhetorical question, but he felt this was the one place where he could help.

"Why would you? Most people aren't pretending to be someone they aren't," he said, hoping to reassure her.

"Are they? Most people are putting on an image that they want to see. Heck, I even do it—successful IT girl, boss babe. When in truth, I'm covering up the hot mess that I truly am," she said. "But I do try to make sure that I don't hurt anyone."

He normally did too. "This situation—"

"Please. I know you have some justifiable truth to tell me and if you let me calm down I might be able to hear it. But at this moment, I can only react as my worst self."

"That's okay. I can handle your worst," he murmured.

"I'm not sure *I* can," she said. "The last time a man did this to me, it took me years to find myself again and I don't have that luxury this time. I have a business that is on the cusp of going national and I'm not going to let you derail me."

"Good for you."

She lifted an eyebrow. "You sound condescending."

"I'm not trying to be. I don't want to see you fail. I like your success, I like your dreams and your version of the future," he said.

He had to wonder if that was why he'd kept quiet and not told her the truth about himself sooner. The dreams she had of a life together weren't ones that Sean O'Neill could fit in to.

"My version...well, it's different now," she said as Lyle pulled to a stop in front of her building. He started to reach for the door but she shook her head at him.

"Don't get out."

"When can I see you again?" he asked.

"I'll text you."

Lyle opened her door and offered her his hand, and Paisley took it, getting out of the car without a backward glance. The driver escorted her to the door of her building and Paisley disappeared inside. He could only watch her go and he knew that he had to make a choice. Either fix this and find a way to win her back or...let her go.

* * *

Paisley walked through her apartment like she was in a trance. She kicked off her shoes, dropped her cloak and bag on the floor and just kept moving, but she didn't know where she was going. Swallowing past the lump in her throat, she unzipped her evening dress, then let it sit where it had fallen and started to put on the sweats she'd been using when she worked from home. But they had been Jack's. The tears she had been holding back finally started to fall, and she let it all out.

She'd *trusted* him. Or come as close to trusting a man as she could, but this… She should have seen it coming. Except she'd thought she'd been wise.

Paisley walked into her bedroom, ignoring the unmade bed where they'd made love that morning, and went to her walk-in closet. She found a clean pair of leggings and her favorite *Nightmare Before Christmas* sweatshirt.

After throwing them on, she sank down on the floor, drew her knees up to her chest and rested her forehead on them. She was so mad. Like she wished she could punch him in his perfect face. How could she have been so stupid? There were so many men in the world and she had to get knocked up by a guy who was pretending to be someone else.

She was glad he wasn't a criminal, but honestly, lying wasn't that much better in her estimation. But it would have been easier. He could have told her the truth.

Paisley angrily scrubbed away her tears. She was so unsure of everything right now. The baby… Another innocent life that she had to protect. She was strong enough to do it—after all, she had protected her younger siblings when she'd been growing up. But a part of her had started to think maybe she wouldn't have to always be the one keeping everyone safe.

Why, oh, why had she let him into her life?

She'd started to feel like she'd finally shed the skin of the girl she'd been. That she had finally become a woman who was strong enough to make smart decisions. Yet now…all her old self-doubt came crawling back. For the first time, she had an inkling of how her mom had found herself married to a con man. And she finally had some sympathy for her mother.

Her doorbell rang, but she didn't want to see anyone. Not now.

The doorbell chimed again, followed by loud pounding, and then she heard the door open.

"Pais? Where are you?"

Olive. With a weary sigh, she pushed herself to her feet. At least she didn't have to put up a brave front with Olive. She could just be herself.

She walked to her bedroom doorway and saw Delaney following Olive through the front door, using the key she'd given both of them in case of emergency. Neither of them said a word—they just walked over to her and hugged her. She cried even harder as her best friends embraced her. Her heart was broken, her trust shattered and her self-confidence at an all-time low as she stood there, but they had faith in her, loved her and made her feel better.

"I feel so stupid and mad."

"You're not stupid," Delaney said. "But I'm pissed too. He's about to see just how crazy the Dish Soap Heiress really is."

"Stop it, Dellie. This is Paisley's pain, not yours," Olive pointed out. "We brought ice cream, vodka and cranberry juice…and our pj's."

"Thanks. I can't drink."

"That's right, you're pregnant," Delaney said.

"Yeah, I am."

"Fuck," Delaney said.

"Oh," Olive said at the same time.

Then they both stepped back to look at her. The sympathy in their eyes made her feel…well, certainly not great. "I know. It wasn't planned and now I'm shook. I mean the guy I thought I knew doesn't even exist."

"Jerk. What do you need? Obviously, we will be by your side through this entire thing. I did think he was too good to be true," Olive said as she went into the kitchen and started dishing up ice cream. "But I hoped I was wrong."

"Me too," Delaney added.

"He was really great, wasn't he? But I think it was just a part he was playing for a role," Paisley said as she sank down onto the couch.

Delaney sat down next to her, putting her arm around Paisley's shoulder.

"Not to be crass…but are you keeping the baby?" Delaney asked.

"Yes. I mean from the moment I realized I was pregnant, I just wanted the baby. Even knowing he lied to me, I still want the child."

It was like from the moment that she'd confirmed it she knew she wouldn't be alone anymore. She would have a little human that she could nurture and trust. Her mom had been unreliable growing up because she had covered for Paisley's dad as a way to try to protect Paisley and her siblings. But lies always came to the surface. However, with this baby, she could have the family she'd always wanted. She was going to have someone in her life whom she could love unconditionally, and after tonight, she needed that more than ever.

"We are going to be the best aunties any baby ever had," Delaney promised. "And the best support you could ask for."

Olive handed them all bowls of rocky road ice cream, then sat down on Paisley's other side. "What about Jack… I mean, Sean? It's odd to think of him as someone other than Jack."

"I know. I haven't told him about the baby. I just need space to deal with his news."

"Of course, you couldn't," Olive murmured. "Delaney and I can handle anything that comes up if you need a few days off."

"No. I'm going to be working as normal. It's the holiday season and I have a few clients who need to make the most of the season of giving to help their images," Paisley said. She had to focus on work. Because right now she knew that was the only way she was going to get over Sean and her broken heart. She wasn't going to let him take anything more from her.

Her friends were going to stay the night. Delaney made her laugh by sharing a story of how she and her fiancé, Nolan, had been interrupted while making love by his six-year-old daughter, Daisey. Meanwhile, Olive washed the sheets on her bed and put everything of Sean's in a box, then stuck it near the door.

She knew she should be grateful for her friends and they lightened her mood, but she needed to be alone to plan her way out of this. To pretend that her broken heart would mend and that she was going to be okay again. Because right now it sure felt like she wouldn't be.

Sitting alone in his hotel room, Sean knew he needed a new script for himself and Paisley, but another part of him knew that what she needed was the real man. Not a part he was playing. And he'd never been good at that. He had grown up in front of the camera and embodying whatever role he was given had always been easy for him.

His career had started at age six and it had taken him years of therapy to realize that the connections he had when the camera was rolling had felt more real than his relationship with his television-character-actor mother.

That first role had been with his mom on her series, but soon he caught fire with the audience and he became the breakout star. His relationship with his mother had never been the same, since Sean's fortunes continued to grow and hers waned.

His phone rang and he glanced at the screen to see it was his agent, Thom Mulholland. They'd both been child actors together until Thom had followed in his dad's footsteps and started working at his entertainment agency.

He answered the video call, propping up his phone on the bottle of Jack Daniel's that he'd opened when he'd gotten back to his room.

"Dude, you are screwed. Is that the girl you've been living with?"

"Thanks, Thom. I already figured that out," Sean grumbled.

"Just saying that photo of the two of you is already all over the place. And she looks…well, let's just say I wouldn't want to be in your shoes."

"Yeah, me, either."

"So what's next?" Thom asked.

"I don't know." He blew out a frustrated breath. "I mean, I can't just channel another role—Paisley would never forgive me."

"So be yourself."

"No one likes the real me."

"I do," his agent said. "Except when you let your ego take over."

"Why am I friends with you?"

"Because I keep it real," Thom said.

"I could do with a little less realism and some sympathy, and maybe a plan."

Thom leaned back in his chair, and behind him, Sean could see the windows that he knew overlooked the Pacific Ocean. Thom tended to work out of his Malibu mansion.

"Write this girl off and come home. You'll do press for the new movie and then come February, you go to Vancouver to start filming again. Work is always the answer."

Sean shook his head. Work wasn't going to fix this. He needed to make things right with Paisley. He'd hurt her and hadn't meant to. But in all honestly, he had barely allowed himself to think about that. "She's pissed, but I can't leave until I make things right with her."

"Fu-u-uck."

Instead of answering Thom, Sean drained his glass and then shifted the phone to refill it. Getting drunk was starting to seem like his new plan.

"What are you going to do? Want me to help? I could come out there and talk to her."

"No. You're not doing that."

Thom grimaced. "So…what do you want with this girl—"

"Stop calling her that," Sean snapped. "Her name is Paisley."

His agent put up his hands. "Okay, okay. I'm just trying to watch your back, like I always do."

"I appreciate that…" Sean said.

"But?"

"I screwed up. I let her think I was Jack, my movie persona, and I want to fix this. She's not the kind of woman who lets just anyone in."

Thom rolled his eyes at that statement, and Sean shook his head. "She's not."

"You sound defensive. Women always know who you are."

"She thought I was some low-rent guy who may or may not be a criminal." Her standing by him was part of the reason why he wanted to make this right. Paisley had supported him, tried to urge him into better life choices and made him feel like he mattered. Even though he knew he wasn't the aimless man she'd seen him as, he couldn't help but feel moved by what she'd tried to do for him.

"Okay. So what can I do? The studio wants you to do press and explain the gir— Paisley."

"I don't want her to be a part of this," Sean said firmly.

"Too late. Her face is going to be everywhere and once they find out that you lied to her—"

"They can't. I don't want that to get out, Thom. And I want her name kept out of the press. Take care of that."

"I will. Who knows besides you two?"

"Her friends, but they won't say anything," Sean said. "Can you get the studio to hire a Chicago-based brand-imaging consultant for me?"

"You know I can. Who do you want?"

"IDG," he replied. "And I want Paisley Campbell to be the one in charge of it."

"Paisley runs this brand-image company?"

"She does."

"I'm finding it harder to believe she didn't recognize you," Thom said.

"Not everyone is a schemer. She has a thing about honesty. Trust me, she didn't know. You said you saw her face in the photo," Sean reminded him.

Thom started typing on his laptop keyboard while they were talking. "I did. Okay, let me get this rolling. Do you want to do press and everything in Chicago?"

"Yes. Like I said, I have to stay and fix this."

"Fine." Thom blew out a breath. "Let me work it from this end. I'll get back to you."

"Thanks."

"No problem." Then he gave Sean a smug look. "I know you don't want to hear it, but it's about time something shook up your life."

He flipped his friend the bird and disconnected the call while Thom was laughing. Then he walked over to the windows that looked down on Michigan Avenue. He'd been in Chi-Town for months and hadn't done anything touristy after a few close calls with some fans. He'd laid low and learned what it was like to have a normal life with Paisley.

Sean had felt both at home and constrained by that lifestyle. Maybe it was good that she knew who he was. He knew that he could never live her kind of quiet life; he needed excitement and adrenaline to help keep him in control. But he had no idea how he was going to find that with her. He only knew he had to try.

Four

Paisley looked at the email offer for the third time after having deleted the message and then retrieving it from the trash folder. From a clearheaded business standpoint, there was no question that she should be typing back a *yes*. In fact, she should have already responded. Yet, despite the fact that this offer had come from a huge Hollywood studio and the contract had huge dollar signs tied to it, she was hesitating.

She didn't want to be the brand consultant and image manager for Sean O'Neill on his big-budget holiday film. But on the other hand, she *did* want the Hollywood contact as she'd been trying to grow IDG and move them from a regional firm into a national one. Something she was hyperaware that

Sean knew. She'd spent too many nights curled in his—or rather, Jack's—arms, talking about her future dreams with him.

So did she spite herself and turn it down because she was still mad at him? Or did she somehow figure out how to be the bigger person and agree to it, represent him and then move on? The money would be good and she had the baby to think of now. The company was doing well enough that she didn't have to worry about money, but still, the connection to Hollywood could open doors for IDG.

Obviously, she should choose the second option, but how was she going to convince herself—and him—that she was over him? Because honestly, it had only been three days. And it had taken her ten years to feel normal after her dad had left them. This was just—

"Morning. Got you an herbal peppermint tea instead of coffee since you're preggers and I wasn't sure about caffeine," Olive said as she walked into the office and set the to-go carrier with three cups in it on Paisley's desk.

"Thanks," she said distractedly. Paisley wasn't sure about the coffee thing, either. Seemed there were conflicting theories on whether one cup a day was fine for the baby or not.

"You okay?" Olive asked. Her friend was wearing a pair of checkered slim-fitting pants and a cream-colored silk blouse with a bow neatly tied at her neck. She had her hair pulled back into a low bun and was wearing a pair of glasses, which Paisley knew she didn't need for reading, to complete the look.

"I got an offer from a Hollywood studio to be brand-image consultant on *Christmas Magic*."

Olive leaned her hip against the desk and took a sip of her coffee and Paisley imagined her friend was trying to think of what to say. Finally, Olive put down her cup. "Want me to take it?"

"Yes, can you? But I thought you had Dante's Christmas promo and your normal clients."

"I do. But this is a big opportunity. Maybe I can get Dante's assistant to help out," Olive said.

"Help out with what?" Delaney asked as she walked into the office. She grabbed the remaining coffee cup from the carrier and took a delicate sip from it.

"IDG got an offer to work with the film and actors from *Christmas Magic*," Paisley told her.

"That bastard!" Delaney huffed. "I mean, I can admire that he is offering you a really big carrot, but still."

"My thoughts exactly. I don't want to turn it down," she said, realizing that it was the truth. They had all been working hard to get to this point. A part of her didn't want Sean to disrupt her life plan any further.

"I'd offer to take it but I've got the museum thing and it's really taking a lot of extra time," Delaney said. "Can you handle it on your own, Paisley?"

"There's no reason I can't," she said. "I'm a grown woman—"

"No one doubts that. But I'm pretty sure it will mean working with Sean. Are you ready for that?" Olive asked.

There it was, the million-dollar question that she was avoiding answering. It was easy to sit her and stew in her anger. To think of how he'd lied to her and how livid she was, but beneath that was something more. Something that made her realize she might never be ready to see him again. She still liked Jack. She still wanted the man that Sean had pretended to be for herself and the baby. Those thoughts made her doubt herself in a way she never had before.

She'd always prided herself on being strong. She was the friend who gave the hard advice and then had the other person's back. But even though she knew what she'd tell herself to do in this situation, she couldn't deny how she really felt.

Moving on wasn't what she wanted. But continuing anything with Sean would make her feel like the biggest loser in the world. Because the truth was, it was humiliating to think that she might want to work things out with a man who'd lied to her in such a big way.

"You know it's okay to say no," Olive said gently.

Paisley nodded. "I don't know if I'm ready. Part of me thinks it might help me get over him," she admitted. "Or let me see the real man."

Delaney sighed and then shook her head. "I hate

to say this, because I know it's not helpful, but I liked him when we hung out. There was that one awkward thing when I asked about his grandmother which now I totally get. But otherwise… I mean, I know he's an actor and all, but it felt real. Do you think he wasn't being his true self with you?"

"I just don't know," she said, glancing down at the email and the initial figure they'd offered her. It was big. But money wasn't enough of a motivation for her. Deep down, she knew she wanted to find out more about Sean. To see who he really was and to find out if he'd just used her. And work might give her a safe space to do that. "I'm going to say yes. If it doesn't work out, I can walk away."

"Or one of us will step in," Olive said. "But in any event, I think you should set some boundaries for yourself with Sean."

"Good idea," she agreed. What should the ground rules be? Well, first and foremost, no lies. And she also needed to know what kind of man the father of her child was. The headlines and his reputation didn't really paint a good picture of the type of guy she wanted to raise a baby with. Yet Jack had been different. A quiet, honest man…which she now knew was a lie. She needed to know who Sean O'Neill *really* was beyond the public persona and if she could trust him to co-parent her child with her.

Sean had no real idea of what Paisley wanted from him. He thought maybe he should do the humble thing and try to win her forgiveness. Except he'd never been humble. And the more he tried to come up with ideas that fit that way of thinking, the more he realized that it wasn't going to work. He wasn't going to be all "sorry, ma'am"—that wasn't who he was.

He'd screwed up and he knew it. He couldn't change it, and even if he could, he doubted he would have. He had liked the quiet life he'd had with Paisley. It had kind of felt like playing house, and as a man who'd always been moving on to the next big thing, it had been a nice reprieve.

But it was over. He wasn't that simple man he'd been portraying and it was time for Paisley to meet the *real* Sean.

To that end, he'd demanded her company do the press and promotional events for the movie and he'd gotten a text from his agent overnight confirming she'd accepted.

That made him realize that boldness was the only way to go with this woman. Sean took care getting dressed for the meeting with her. He'd shaved because he knew that it would accentuate his strong jawline. And he'd styled his hair the way he usually did when he wasn't filming, with some extra product to create a look that suggested he was tousled, but in the best way. As for his attire, he'd pulled out a Hugo Boss suit that he'd received when he'd done a photo shoot with them back in October, when he'd told Paisley he'd been visiting his sick grandmother.

To be honest, when he looked back on his actions,

he realized that he had known she wasn't going to just seamlessly slide back into his Hollywood life. But he did wish he'd been able to break it to her himself.

He took a last look in the mirror and knew he had dressed to woo her as he strode out of his hotel suite. He had his team looking for a house for him to rent near Paisley so that he could move out of the hotel. Part of him wanted to get her to come back to Hollywood with him, but he knew better than to ask. At least right now.

Sean's car was waiting and he walked through the lobby slowly, aware of the many stares that were on him. He smiled at fans, stopped to sign autographs and pose for selfies, then he was in the car and on his way to Paisley's office. Michigan Avenue was decorated for the holidays and though he usually did his best to stay busy so he didn't have to face the truth that he was alone, this year he felt like his world had sort of crashed into Paisley's.

Normally he wouldn't have done all this holiday-themed press, but he wanted Paisley and doing press with her company was the only way he could make her talk to him. And while he wasn't sure if they had anything that would last, he needed to be back in control of their relationship and he wasn't going to settle for anything less.

The driver pulled up in front of the building where her offices were and Sean waited for him to open the door, then got out and let the man know he'd text when he was ready to be picked up. He entered the building, signed in and got on the elevator to go up to her office. A feminine hand stopped the doors from closing and Paisley stepped on, a friendly smile on her face as she looked up. It dropped the moment she realized he was the passenger.

He reached around her to hit the button to close the elevator door and then turned to face her. The flowery scent of her perfume surrounded him and he couldn't stop staring at her mouth. It felt like it had been months since he'd held her in his arms.

They were alone for the first time since that paparazzo had ambushed him and Sean wanted a chance to win back some of the trust he'd lost by not getting to tell her the truth. He knew she was still upset with him.

That made perfect sense, but he wanted her back. He couldn't say if it was emotion driving him, but he suspected it was lust. He knew that he connected with her through their bodies and right now his instinct was to get her back into bed so he could start to make this right.

"I hear we are going to be working together," he murmured.

"We are. I didn't realize you were going to be here. I think we have a Zoom meeting set up—"

"We do," he said. "But I figured it'd be silly for me to do it from my hotel when your office was close."

"Next time please check with me first," she said primly, pulling her red wool coat closer around her.

"I texted you."

"Oh. That's right. I guess put 'work' in the message heading so I'll know to read it."

She was playing it cool and he didn't blame her at all. He got it. But he wasn't going to settle for that. He hit the elevator's stop button and turned to face her.

"Let's clear the air. I'm sorry. I know I've already said that, but I want to make this right," he said.

"You can't."

He frowned at her. "Not if you aren't going to let go of your pride."

"*Pride?* You lied to me for months!"

"I did. But I'm not now and eventually you're going to have to let it go," he said gently. "I mean, you can treat me the way we both know I deserve, or you can be the bigger person and let it go."

"The bigger person? I don't want to be. You're right. I am going to have to move on, but right now—"

She broke off and then reached around him, hitting the button to make the elevator car go again.

"'Right now' what?" he asked as the doors opened on her floor and he gestured for her to step off first.

"Right now I'm still mad. I thought I could separate working with you and what happened…but honestly, I don't know if I can," she admitted as they got off the elevator. "I think I'm going to have to cancel this contract."

He could see the fury in her. Mostly in the way she kept clenching her hands into fists as she stood there talking to him. Also, she wouldn't make eye contact, which she normally always did. He hated that he'd done this to her. This was precisely why he'd always avoided being with someone like Paisley.

Yet despite everything, he felt his cock stir, his skin grew too tight for his body, and he was holding on to his control by a thread. He wanted to lean in and kiss her. Turn that anger he sensed seething in her into passion. Give them both a chance to express what they were trying to keep hidden.

Two people who were real and who didn't hide their emotions. She wore them for the entire world to see and now he had to decide if he could do the same. And if not, he should be the bigger person and walk away. But he knew that he wouldn't.

Paisley hated that she still wanted him and that she had let him get to her. Why couldn't she stop dwelling on the fact that with the stubble on his strong jaw, she could easily see why he'd been named the "Sexiest Man of the Year" twice. Or help but remember how kissing him always made her weak in the knees?

Gah! She'd had a plan to stay cool, but just being in his presence was making her temperature flare, which made her want to do something to hurt him the way he'd hurt her. And that was proof positive why she *shouldn't* be working with him. Because revenge had never been her thing. She'd had never been a mean girl; she had always been the one who took care of everyone else. Who always put herself last. But now that she was pregnant, she couldn't keep doing that.

She'd met Olive and Delaney when they'd all been doing community service—Olive for bullying some of her sorority sisters and Delaney for driving under the influence. Paisley had been there trying to undo some of the bad karma she felt she'd unwittingly attracted when she realized her father had paid for her college tuition with money he'd bilked some elderly widows out of. They'd started their business to use their energy and knowledge for good.

This was—

"Paisley, I am sorry," Sean said again, jerking her out of her thoughts.

She sighed in frustration. How many times was she going to listen to him say it? She pivoted to face him and shook her head. "I know. I'm not ready to forgive."

He nodded. "Fair enough."

He was being so…reasonable. Which, for some reason, was irritating her even more.

"Listen, I won't stay angry forever, but you didn't give me a chance to come to you. You forced this meeting."

"How did I force you?" he asked defensively.

"You dangled a carrot—"

Another elevator car stopped on their floor and the door opened. Paisley grabbed his hand and pulled him down the hall into her office. She tried to ignore the tingle that went through her body at his touch. She wasn't doing this again.

Work with him, get him out of her system—that was the plan.

She closed the door after they were both in the office and leaned back against it, tipping back her head and closing her eyes while she took a deep breath.

"I just didn't want you to close me out. I've seen you do it when you decide to move on," he said.

She looked over at him, surprised by the raw sincerity in his voice. But should she be? "How can I believe anything you say?"

The words were sort of mean, but she couldn't help herself. He'd lied to her, and as much as she knew he had his reasons, she was struggling to forgive him. And if she was being totally honest, she was struggling to forgive herself too for not seeing it. Was this what her mom had felt each time her father had made a promise and then broken it?

"I don't know," he said slowly. "Maybe take a chance and get to know me."

His offer was way too tempting, but she knew she wasn't going to take it. She was the sort of person who thought "fool me once, shame on you—fool me twice, shame on me." However, they had to work together and that was something she could focus on. Also she did want to know what kind of man Sean was. She'd accepted his offer and now she needed to make the most of it.

"Well, I will be getting to know the professional

you," she said. "Let's talk about that. Your film company wants you to do some events that mirror the movie, so we've got singing carols at the Bean, working in the soup kitchen, a weekend stint in the suburbs dressed as Santa and handing out presents."

He made a face. The Bean was a local Chicago attraction tourists flocked to for photos.

"What?"

"Uh, I don't usually do that kind of stuff," he said gruffly.

"I know. The studio knows as well, but you insisted they hire my firm so they wanted to make sure they got their money's worth. I think there is also a high-ticket charity gala that you will host."

"Is that all?"

"So far," she said, realizing that she was enjoying seeing him so uncomfortable. "Today's Zoom is to finalize the list and get approval."

He tipped his head to the side, studying her. She was going to make him jump through hoops and see how far he would let her push him until he put his foot down.

"Okay. How about instead of me being a mall Santa, I host a dinner with Santa for low-income kids and give them a gift off their wish list?"

"Love that idea," she said. "In fact, I think we can partner with the hotel you're staying at to host the event."

She walked past him to her desk so she could write this down. She always thought better with a pen in hand. He stopped her with his hand on her elbow and that sensual shiver went through her again.

"What?"

"Thank you."

He was so close that she felt the soft brush of his minty breath against her cheek and she stared into his piercing blue eyes, wondering how she'd never noticed the tiny flecks of green in them before. His eyes were the most familiar part of him to her. But even *they* were different. Instinctively, she put her forehead on his shoulder, seeking comfort, before she realized what she was doing and turned away.

"This is what I'm paid to do," she said, shrugging out of her coat and draping it on the back of her chair. Then she sat down and pulled her notepad to her.

He didn't say anything as she made notes, then took off his coat, walked back to her desk and leaned one hip against her desk as he watched her. She pretended to be nonchalant and didn't pay any attention to him.

She shook her head and looked over at him. "You are right that I have to move on and as much as I don't approve of your methods, this might help."

He arched one eyebrow. "I'm sort of known for being difficult to work with so this might help more than you expect."

"I'm sort of known for wrangling divas so I think we'll be well matched."

"Diva?"

"You prefer 'spoiled brat'?"

"No. I'm not either."

She ignored him and the smile that teased her lips. Okay, she liked this situation. She had the power and she needed it after the way she'd felt so used by him. But she cautioned herself to remember that he'd lied once. So convincingly that he'd fooled a lot of people, not just her.

What was it that made him so good at that? She knew he was an actor but suspected it was something more. He'd been so natural at it. It worried her that there might not be a real man behind the mask for her to get to know.

Five

Sean knew he needed to be himself and, as always, that induced a level of panic that had him scrolling through characters he'd played over the years, trying to find the right one, but nothing felt right.

"I'm not really comfortable in the diva role," he said.

"Really?" she asked. "Why not?"

He walked over to one of the guest chairs and sat down, not looking at her as he did so. He had one clear memory of being a bragging youngster at home, telling his mom he didn't have to listen to her, since he was the star of *Ranger Ten* and that he didn't have to do chores. Yeah, that hadn't gone well.

One of the few things his mom had taught him

was to be humble about his talent. "Let's just say ten-year-old me liked to strut around and tell everyone he was the star of a TV show."

She put her hands together as she studied him. "How'd that go over?"

"My mom set me straight," he said. He winced at the memory. No one liked someone as successful as he was who whined about their childhood. The fact that his mom hadn't been Mother of the Year didn't really matter now. She'd been out of his life for a long time and they were both happier for it.

"That's nice," she said.

There was a note in Paisley's voice that made him take notice. "Isn't it?"

"Yeah."

"Was your mom like that?"

"No. She was in love and would do anything to try to keep my dad happy," she said, then shook her head. "But we don't have time to unpack that."

She stood up and started walking toward her office door, but he was right behind her and planted his hand on the door so she couldn't open it. She turned, so close that he felt the brush of her body against his as she looked up at him with those wide blue-gray eyes of hers.

"Sean."

"Paisley, you can't say something like that and expect me to ignore it," he said. "You always made your family seem—"

"Perfect. I know. I lied."

"Why?" he asked softly.

"Hmm… I suppose I did it because my upbringing was rough and messy, and I didn't want you to see that in me," she said.

Same, he thought, but didn't say that. "Fair enough. My mom beat me with a belt after I bragged. She told me I wasn't special—I was just lucky. That I'd been cast as Ranger because he made me the boy that she wished I was."

He dropped his arm, stepping back. He certainly hadn't mean to say that.

"Oh, Sean," Paisley said, coming forward and wrapping her arms around him.

For a minute he let himself enjoy her touch. He pulled her closer, breathing in the scent of Paisley. He'd missed her but he knew it was only her soft heart making her hug him now. That little boy he'd been had reached her, but the man standing next to her hadn't.

"She was right. And you are too. We all are just trying to show the world our best sides, skimming over the bad stuff like it isn't there."

He opened the door for her but she stood there for too long. Finally, he looked up at her and saw something in her eyes that resonated deep inside of him. Some kind of mixture of caring, empathy and the kind of knowledge that he wished she didn't have. She touched his hand, just a quick squeeze of his wrist.

"We can talk about us later," she said.

Sean nodded, afraid to say anything else. He felt too raw at this moment. When he got like this, he had to keep a tight lid on himself. He didn't want to lose control around her. So far she'd seen the best side of Sean—that's what Jack had been. Him at his best.

He followed her down the hall, mulling over the fact that she wanted to know who he really was deep down inside. Unfortunately, that man was f-ed up and always had been. That one beating hadn't shaped him into who he was today but it had definitely started his journey. What did it say about him that his best friend was his agent? That his live-in girlfriend thought he was another man? And that he wasn't sure how to be himself and still be likable?

That had always been a big problem for him.

Was he stubbornly staying here in Chicago, trying to mend fences with Paisley, because she was special? Or was it just that he was still trying to prove that Sean O'Neill was as worthy of love as any character he played?

It was all too much for first-thing-in-the-morning thoughts. Those were the kind that he normally saved for late nights after a bottle of Jack Daniels. He welcomed the distraction when she led him into a conference room with a large video monitor at one end. He saw his agent's logo on one of the four squares and then the film poster on another one.

"We'll sit here so they can see us," Paisley explained, gesturing to the two chairs she'd set up at a round table. "This remote will mute our audio so they can't hear us. And this one pauses our video. Do you want a coffee or water, or something else?"

"Water would be good," he said. "Is it just us and Thom Mulholland and the marketing team?"

"No, your leading lady, Desi Jones, is going to be on as well," she told him. "I have our company logo up right now on their screens. If anyone comes on while I'm gone, you can activate the camera with this button. I'll get your water and be right back."

He watched her leave, thinking that she'd softened a bit toward him. Was it just that she felt sorry for him because of his childhood? He knew that was a turn-on for some woman and had exploited it in the past. But Paisley didn't seem the type.

In fact, he was forced to consider it was the fact that he'd shared the truth with her. She seemed to be a truth warrior and as much as he hated his past, he might have to tap in to it if he was going to figure out why he wasn't ready to move on from her.

Paisley realized as the meeting ended with the film company that the white-hot anger she'd felt toward Sean had sort of dampened as he followed her back into her office. Delaney gave him the stink eye when she walked past and muttered, "Asshole."

"Nice to see you too, Delaney."

She just gave him the finger and kept walking. Olive's office door was closed, something that Paisley was thankful for. She loved that her friends had her back, but as her feelings for Sean were starting to morph into something different, she wasn't too sure what to do next.

She was no longer furious with him. Which didn't seem like a good thing to her.

But she had also realized that she still knew nothing of the real man. Jack had been down-to-earth, sort of a rough-and-tumble guy who acted on his impulses. Sean, on the other hand, was urbane and witty. Smarter than Paisley had guessed and able to use his charm to get his way. As evidenced, she thought, by the very fact that she was working with him. No one told Sean O'Neill *no* or if they did, he found a way to change it to a *yes*.

Sean's charm was something that she didn't trust, not just because she'd been falling for Jack, but because of their baby. She needed to be very sure of him before she told him about the child.

She should just keep it all business, she reminded herself. He was a client now, not a man whose body she'd seen naked and knew as well as her own. She needed remember that the man in front of her was a movie star. Someone whom she normally would have no chance with…

But as he casually sat in her guest chair, his long, muscular legs stretched out in front of him, it was hard not to recall going down on him in this very office a little over a month ago. And then he'd pulled her up on his lap and taken her hard and fast. She felt her face getting hot and turned to look out the windows. The day was that icy, rainy, drab December that no one really wanted. Yet to her, it was the perfect day to cuddle close under the covers and make love.

"Did I bring too much drama?" he asked.

She took a deep breath, shaking off the vestiges of the erotic image in her mind, and faced him. "No, but then I'm beginning to realize that you do use charm to get your way instead of throwing your weight around."

"Well," he said with a sardonic grin. "I learned the hard way that getting everyone's cooperation is easier than stomping my foot."

Except he didn't seem like the kind of man to stomp his foot until he got his way. "Well, I guess you should head back to your hotel, while I reach out to my contacts and get everything set up. I have your number…or should I go through your assistant?"

She'd been surprised when his assistant had shown up on the video call. Bert was a young-looking thirty, with wiry dark hair and a very laid-back feel. He had just taken notes, interjected with things he'd handle and asked if he should come to Chicago or stay at Sean's place in Malibu. Which Sean said they'd discuss later.

"Let me talk to Bert," Sean said. "This is just between us but I think he was planning to propose to his long-term girlfriend at Christmas so I don't want him out here if that interferes."

"Okay. I'll copy him on everything so he's in the

loop," she replied, trying not to let the fact that he was putting his assistant in front of himself affect her thoughts of who he was. Yet she had to. This was what she had wanted, why she'd agreed to take him on as a client. She needed to know the man behind the headlines for both herself and her baby. If she decided to cut Sean out of their lives, she owed her child the truth about its father.

"Perfect. Now then, what about lunch?"

She quirked an eyebrow. "What about it?"

"Will you go to lunch with me?"

"No," she said. She had a fire to put out with a local celebrity chef.

"I thought you wanted to get to know me."

"I do, but you're not my only client. I have someone who I need to go see," she told him primly. "I am available for coffee at three if you want to meet me at the shop where we first met."

He pushed himself to his feet and came over to her desk, holding out his hand.

She stared at it for a long moment, and when she finally took it, he bent, brushing his lips against the back of hers. "It's a date."

"Not a date—a *business* meeting," she insisted. But the shiver of sensual awareness that went through her made that lie apparent. She was never going to be blasé about Sean touching her.

"See you later," he said with a wink, then walked out of her office and closed the door behind him.

After he left, she leaned back in her chair and let out a breath she hadn't been aware she was holding. This was getting more complicated.

Honestly, she would have been happier if he'd been the asshole that Delaney had labeled him. But he was more than that. She was starting to realize that Jack was just one thin layer of the man that Sean was. This professional movie star was another layer. And the child with the abusive mom another one. But how did they all come together and who was the *real* Sean O'Neill?

She'd given herself these two weeks to find out.

But would that be enough time? A part of her wasn't entirely sure that a lifetime would be enough to figure him out.

And more importantly, she thought, how was she going to balance the idea that she still wanted him and he didn't know she was pregnant with his child?

She had no clue. Before she could ponder that problem any further, her phone vibrated and she looked down to see it was a message from Sean.

Thanks for giving me a second chance.

Is that what I'm doing?

I hope so.

We'll see. <smiley face> Later.

She put down her phone and dove into her other client, who was an *actual* drama king, and tried not to think about second chances. They'd rarely worked in her experience, but she was hoping that this time maybe things would work out.

Bert texted him that he'd found a house for Sean to use instead of the hotel. He was having it cleaned, decorated and brought up to Sean's specifications. Bert thought that he should be able to move in that evening.

He called his assistant to verify. "Hey, Bert. Tonight?"

"Yeah. I mean, I threw your name around and a lot of money toward them and they said they'd have it ready. It's already furnished, so that part's easy. I'm just having them tweak things the way you like them. I emphasized the need for secrecy and that the tabloid press were all over you like a rash," Bert said with a chuckle.

"Thanks for that. Also, I told Paisley to liaise with you, but that I don't want you to have to come out here."

"I appreciate that," he murmured. "I'm still not sure when I'm going to pop the question, but being in LA will make the timing easier. Also…well, I know you don't have family, so Christa and would like you to join us for Christmas this year. I know you have to stay in Chicago to do the press for the movie and all so, we'll come to you."

Sean was touched. Normally he and Bert went to an island he owned in the Caribbean for the holidays. They'd always spent it together because, in essence, they were alone. And Christa, who worked for a local television station as a news anchor, couldn't travel. So he knew they were making a lot of sacrifices to ensure he wouldn't be alone. He also knew that it was all down to Bert finding him that one year stoned out of his head on the twenty-sixth.

"I'm good. You don't have to—"

"I know that, man. I'm doing this as your friend. And we both know you've been there for me, so it's the least I can do. And as I said, it was Christa's idea," Bert said. "I can't tell her you said no, she'll think you don't like her."

Bert was making it easy for him to agree. And as he had no family other than Bert and his agent, maybe he should go along with the plan. "You know I like her—she makes you a better man."

"That she does," Bert said. "We'll be landing on the twenty-third and we are staying until New Year's. The place I got you has a guesthouse in the back, so we'll stay there. Okay?"

"Yes, thank you, Bert. I'm not like I was back then," he reminded him. For a few years he'd been taking roles that exacerbated his darker impulses. The roles had netted him Oscar nominations and a Golden Globe win, but the toll on his psyche had been high.

"Dude, you're like my bro. I know you're not in

that place. But it's the holidays and I want to spend it with the people who mean the most to me."

"Me too," he said, realizing for the first time that he might be ready to trust in the close-knit bond that he and Bert had forged together. They were like brothers and Sean had been mentoring his assistant and helping him as he tried to get into production. Bert wanted to direct and together they'd been looking for the right project for him. Sometimes he thought about the found family he'd created for himself. He'd heard that blood was thicker than water, but for Sean it had seemed that wasn't the case. The people he trusted and called family weren't blood.

All of his life he'd substituted the cast and crew on film and TV sets for family, embodying a role and letting himself become that part until it was over. He'd been a nomad for so long he wasn't sure he had it in him to put down roots anywhere, but these last few months with Paisley had shown him another side of himself.

But was wanting enough?

"See you on the twenty-third," he said to Bert as he disconnected the call.

Sean scrubbed a hand across his face. He had spent so much time pretending he wasn't sure he even knew who he really was. However, now, with the stakes higher than ever, never had it been more important that he figure himself out. But…and this was a big one. As touched as he was by Bert and Christa coming to spend Christmas with him, it also made him feel like he was once again pretending to be something he wasn't.

The only thing he knew about being a brother was what he'd learned from roles he'd played. Mentoring…well, that was easier because it was right in his professional wheelhouse. The one place he felt safe.

Letting down Bert and Christa would be easier than letting down Paisley, he admitted.

But was it a sure thing that he would disappoint her?

He shook his head and knew he needed to stop obsessing over this. He wasn't even sure she liked him as Sean. He'd met her when he was so deep in his role that it had been Jack courting her and falling for her.

Now Sean had to step in because he wanted her. He wasn't going to deny it. He liked her clever tongue and cheeky smile. Plus, she was the best lover he'd ever had and he wanted her back in his bed. But he knew that she wasn't after another short-term affair with him. He had to be…the best version of himself. And that was a lot of work.

Was she worth it?

Was *he*?

That floored him—he hadn't realized until that moment that he was always careful to keep himself from making permanent attachments because he knew he didn't feel like he deserved them. A part of him was still that child TV star who'd learned the hard way that the only thing special about him was his TV role.

Six

Sean saw Paisley donned in her long winter coat and carrying her work bag as she entered the coffee shop. Her hair was delectably disheveled, as if it was just after they'd made love. He hardened and shifted his stance to accommodate his erection. He was trying to be chill, but he had no game around Paisley. Maybe if he got her back between the sheets, he might. She glanced around for him and gave him a wave, hurrying over with a harried look on her face. A tendril of hair had escaped her ponytail and curled against her cheek.

"Sorry to do this, but I've had an emergency come up. I can't have coffee with you," she said.

He got to his feet and pulled on his coat, handing

her the mocha he'd ordered for her while he'd been waiting. She smiled her thanks.

"What kind of emergency?"

She took a sip of her coffee and then gave him that sort of sad smile of hers. "A personal one. I really can't stay, but didn't want to text since things have been…well, you know. I didn't want you to think I was just bailing because I didn't want to see you."

He nodded, appreciating her thoughtfulness. But he knew that was the type of woman that Paisley was. "Can I help?"

She tipped her head to the side. "How are you at decorating cookies?"

"Never done it before but that's never stopped me," he said smoothly. "Lead on."

She didn't quibble, which told him that she didn't have the time and could use more hands. When he stepped out of the coffee shop, he noticed she had Lyle, Delaney and Olive waiting in the car. He opened the door to the back seat for Paisley and then got in the front passenger seat next to the driver.

Lyle didn't say a word, just put the car in gear, and drove them to their location. There wasn't any conversation in the back seat, but did hear the tapping of nails on the touch screens and guessed that they were texting about him.

He turned his head and met Olive's steady gaze. Since Delaney had previously given him the finger, it was safe to assume he wasn't their favorite person.

"Hello, ladies, I'm sure you've heard that I'm not really Jack."

"Yeah, we heard," Delaney said in a clipped tone.

"I'm sorry for deceiving you. I was in town for a role and I needed to keep it quiet."

"We get it," Olive said. "We have NDAs that we have to sign all the time. It's the hurting our friend by lying to her while you were sleeping with her that's harder to forgive."

"Olive," Paisley hissed.

"Go, girl!" Delaney said.

"I understand where you both are coming from. I've apologized to her as well. But for today, can we all put that aside and help with Paisley's emergency?"

Olive, who had always been nice to him, nodded. "We all make mistakes and owning them is important."

"I agree."

Delaney sort of huffed and pulled out her phone, looking down at it and ignoring the rest of them.

"So what's the cookie emergency?" he asked.

"Mrs. B, an elderly friend of mine who is decorating cookies for children who are coming here for her group carol tonight, had some cancellations due to flu."

"How many cookies are we talking about?" he asked, deciding to focus on Paisley. She was, after all, the reason he was in this car and going to decorate cookies. He had never done that before. Not even for a role.

"Probably close to five hundred," she said.

That sounded like a ridiculous number of cookies. "For *caroling*?"

"Yes. They work with after-school programs for kids whose parents aren't home in the afternoon. Mrs. B and her group also play secret Santa for the kids. This is one of the many events they hold," Paisley informed him, as Lyle pulled into the underground parking garage of a high-rise apartment building. The driver got out and held the door for Delaney and Sean did the same for Paisley. Olive got out on Delaney's side.

He offered Paisley his hand, which she took, and when their eyes met he felt that sizzle of awareness between them. "Thanks for letting me come along."

She smiled up at him. "Thanks for wanting to."

She tugged her hand free and he closed the door, following her into the building. They went to the third-floor apartment of Mrs. B, and Sean learned her full name was Mildred Buchner. She'd been a teacher for forty years before she retired. She had hair that reminded him of Lucille Ball's, an easy smile and a kind of booming laugh that made everyone take notice.

She took one look at him with a practiced eye. "How many cookies have you decorated?"

"None," he reported.

"Then you go over there with Candace on the snowmen. One big swipe of white frosting seems about your skill level."

"Yes, ma'am," he said, going over to a card table that was set up with large pots of white frosting and stacks of cut-out snowmen-out sugar cookies. "Hi. I'm Sean."

"Candace," the elderly woman returned. "I see you've been delegated to the talentless table."

He laughed. "I have no skills—what about you?"

"Me, either. But Mildred is desperate for help so she called and asked me to assist. I'm known for my slap-and-dash decorating."

"What is slap-and-dash?"

"Slap on the frosting, like so." She picked up a cookie spread a thick bit of frosting all over it and then reached for a jar of sprinkles. "Then dash them with these babies."

She shook the sprinkles over the cookie and then turned and placed it on a tray behind them. "Think you can do that?"

"Yeah, I think so."

She laughed and they worked on the cookies, with Candace talking and telling him stories about the other volunteers in the room. After a while, she stopped talking and looked over at him.

"Most of us are here for Mildred, but I can tell you're here for Paisley."

"I am. She asked and I couldn't say no."

"She has that effect on people." Candace smiled warmly. "Such a good-hearted girl. I wonder sometimes if she goes overboard to make up for her father."

"I don't know who her father is," Sean admitted. She'd only vaguely talked of her siblings and her mom when they'd been together, and since he was hiding some of himself, he hadn't felt like he'd had the right to ask.

"Jeffrey Campbell. He bilked tons of people in the area out of their savings, including Mildred."

Sean's eyes widened, then he looked over at Paisley, thinking that he might not know her at all. There was apparently a lot more to this woman than he'd let himself realize.

Inviting Sean to come to Mrs. B's was a gamble. Paisley always tried to keep this part of her life private, but she was thinking of her baby—*Sean's baby*—and how her life had been two very different worlds. A part of her really wanted to see something in Sean that would convince her he was the man she'd thought she knew. So she'd brought him here.

When he'd gone over to work with Candace, Paisley hadn't known what to expect, but he was working steadily and talking to the old woman like they were lifelong friends. She was torn. She felt like maybe she'd seen in him all the things she wanted to find in a man, but had also been waiting for him to fail, waiting for him to disappoint her. And then, when he had…she'd been hurt, but deep down, not surprised.

"So I thought you were dating a man named Jack," Mrs. B said as they worked on the intricate decorating of the cookies.

"Um…yeah. So, um, Sean *is* Jack."

Mrs. B cleared her throat. "Do I even want to know more?"

"Probably, you're nosy just like me."

Mrs. B laughed and nodded. "I am. Spill."

"He's an actor," she said quietly. He wasn't hiding his identity anymore, but she didn't feel comfortable with that side of him. She wondered if she ever would. Based on her experiences with others, she wasn't sure how much she'd enjoy his fame.

"Is he famous?" Mrs. B asked her.

"Yes, he is."

Mrs. B put down the piping bag of icing and took off her glasses to glance over at Candace and Sean. "I don't recognize him."

"I didn't, either. But he's been the Sexiest Man of the Year twice," she said, laughing for the first time at that fact, hoping that the other woman didn't hear the underlying sadness in it.

Mrs. B put her arm around Paisley. "Don't beat yourself up. We all see what we want to."

"Wise words," she murmured, but given that she was pregnant with a baby by a man she really didn't know was a bit hard to accept. "Thanks."

"You told me the same thing when everything happened with your father. Remember? You said I saw the good in everyone and therefore expected them to live up to that?"

She'd forgotten about that. "I still believe that.

But I should have known better. I mean, given my past, seeing a liar—"

"Maybe he wasn't lying where it counted. You responded to something in him," Mrs. B pointed out.

"Stop making sense! It's just easier to stay mad than to take a chance on..." Caring again and being wrong about him. Her emotions hadn't been rock-solid when it came to Sean. She'd fallen for Jack and only when she'd found out he was Sean did she even have a clue he wasn't who she'd thought he was. What did that say about her?

"Being fooled again. I know. I remember when a certain Campbell came to me and offered to buy me a condo," Mrs. B said.

Paisley looked over at the woman who had become a good friend in the last ten years. Mrs. B had been one of her father's last victims before he'd been arrested and convicted of fraud. He'd bilked her out of her home by having her sign a second mortgage and all of her savings. Her father had defaulted on the loan, of course. Paisley had been horrified when she'd learned that her father had used that money to pay for her college tuition. He'd lied to her and told her he'd turned over a new leaf and gotten a real job... She still felt so much guilt over that.

She was still coming to peace with her part in her father's actions. But she'd used her own credit to buy this condo for Mrs. B. She had done what her conscience had demanded to make reparations.

"I'm glad you trusted me."

"It didn't take me long to realize that you were as sincere as your father was false. You have a good heart, Paisley. I think that man must have something you respond to."

"Sex appeal," Delaney said as she came over to them and hugged Mrs. B.

Her friend wasn't wrong. Paisley remembered the first time she'd met him in line at Hestia's Hearth and Madison had taken his order. Madison was a friend but also a client. She'd felt something electric go through her just because of the timbre of his voice.

"It's hard to tell from here. He's certainly no Robert Redford."

Paisley started laughing and Delaney and Mrs. B joined in. Sean looked over at them and smiled, and deep in her soul she acknowledged she was already starting to forgive him. Mrs. B was right—there was something about this man that resonated with her. And despite what Delaney had said, Paisley hoped it was more than sex.

It *had* to be, she told herself. She needed it to be for her sake and the sake of her unborn child. But when she looked up a few minutes later, Sean was gone. She tried not to take it as a sign but it was hard not to.

Despite Paisley's help, they were running out of time to bake and frost the cookies needed. Sean took a look around, realizing that he had a chance to help her, in a way that had nothing to do with promoting his movie. He refused to let himself dwell on the fact that he probably should have just found a way to stay in Chi-Town that didn't involve work. He left the room to text a chef friend and tell him what they needed. Remy got back to him quickly and hooked him up with a local celebrity chef who could bring over cookies.

He texted the location and then turned as the door behind him opened.

"Hey, I thought you left," Paisley said as she came out. He saw the worry and the disappointment clearly on her gorgeous face.

"Nah, wouldn't let my best girl down when she needed me."

She gave him a skeptical look.

"Just called in a favor. We should have more cookies than you need here in about an hour."

"*What?* How?"

"I've been in touch with Chef Dom Mallon—he's the head chef of the restaurant where I took you for dinner…the other night."

"The night when the jig was up?"

"Yeah, that one," he said with a sheepish grin. "He's got his kitchen baking and frosting cookies, and they'll be here in about an hour and a half. That means Mrs. B and Candace can get ready for their sing-along. Candace has arthritis, by the way, so frosting wasn't easy for her."

"Uh, thank you. Let me tell the ladies. I think

the last batch of cookies in the oven may have been burned."

He nodded. "Yeah, I could tell everyone was starting to panic."

"Wait here."

He did as she asked but took a moment to reach out to Olive's fiancé, Dante, whom he'd met several times for margaritas with the women. He asked the other man to send over some of his Merry Christmas Satan brew for the adults. Dante texted back that he'd be there.

Dude, wish you'd leveled with us.

Me too. Sorry I didn't.

It's cool with me but the girls are pissed.

Believe me, I know. Hopefully this will help.

It might. See ya later.

He was about to go back into Mrs. B's apartment when Delaney came out and walked over to him in that bold way she had. "So you did a nice thing. Thank you."

Then she pulled out her phone and started tapping on the screen as she brushed past him. He had a feeling that he and Delaney weren't going to be besties anytime soon.

Which suited him just fine. He was here for Paisley. For a second chance to see if the last few months had been real or just some residual feeling from the role he'd playing.

The door opened again and Paisley joined him. "Sorry about that. Wanted to let the ladies know they could stop working frantically to bake cookies. They are having cordial and we are invited to join them."

"Sure," he said. Seeing Paisley in this environment was making him want her even more. She'd dropped her guard while they were here, and no longer seemed to be keeping him at arm's length. "Candace mentioned you bought Mrs. B's condo for her."

"I did."

And just like that, she had her defenses up again and was looking at him as if to ask "what of it?" He touched her hand and felt a shiver go through her. She was trying to keep them on some sort of platonic footing, but it was evident she wanted him too. He realized that his lying to her must have been triggering. Sort of putting her right back to that time in her life where she could never trust her father.

"It was a kind gesture. I think too many times people overlook doing those types of things…but not you."

She turned her hand over under his, those magic fingers of hers moving against his palm and sending a bolt of heat up his arm and through his body.

He wanted to concentrate on her words and not on the arousal she stirred so easily in him.

"It was only right. Dad had used the money to pay for my college tuition and expenses. I wouldn't have taken it if I'd known, but he had told me he got a bonus at work… I—I think I hated that I believed him after he'd lied so many times before," she said.

He had the feeling she was letting him know why she was so mad at him and he got it. Truly. He pulled her closer to him, blocking out the rest of the room with his body, and leaned in closer. Her mouth was a temptation he couldn't resist. He brushed his lips against hers, just briefly.

She sighed when he lifted his head.

Suddenly he understood how much his lie had hurt her. Could he make up for it? He should back off for now. He needed to play this right or he was going to lose her.

"So how did you afford to buy Mrs. B's place?"

"After IDG started I put all of my money in savings and used my stake in the company as collateral to get a mortgage for Mrs. B. I pay it off every month," she said. "It's not a big deal."

He thought it was a big deal and that he was learning a lot more about Paisley now than he had over the last few months when they'd been a couple. "Why didn't you ever mention this to me?"

She flushed and chewed her lower lip. "Didn't seem important."

He wanted to run his thumb over her lower lip but kept his hands at his sides. "But it is. Did you come and see Mrs. B without me?" he asked her.

"I did," she said.

"So I wasn't the only one who was hiding part of themselves."

She turned away for a minute and then looked back at him. "Maybe we both were afraid to let our guard down."

"No maybe about it," he said thickly.

"Other than this, I shared everything with you. And…it's not easy when your father is a convicted felon. It's not something I go around talking about."

Something about this conversation was making him remember all the intimate conversations they'd had in her bed. But this was the first time they'd gotten to the truth. He felt more intimate with her now in this room of people than he had when they'd been naked.

He wanted her naked now. Wanted to somehow find a way to put them back on old footing. But he was starting to realize they couldn't go back.

"Like me and my career. Sometimes it's nice to just have a fresh slate and be the person you wish you were," he said. He was leading her a little bit. Trying to make her see that his lie wasn't as intentional as she might have thought. But at the same time, she had obviously sensed something in him that made her not trust him.

He tried to tell himself it wasn't a big thing, but that doubting part of him was very afraid it was. Maybe she'd sensed the same emptiness that he'd always feared was all he had inside.

Seven

Paisley didn't have time to really dwell on everything that Sean had said. But he'd had a point that she'd missed, or maybe *deliberately* missed. She had hidden part of herself from him and she felt more than a twinge of guilt as she realized she was still doing it. The afternoon went by with lots of conversations with the women and she purposefully kept her distance from Sean, watching him to see what else she had missed.

The truth was that he was pretty much acting as he did when he was Jack. Was she making more out of his hidden identity than she should have?

The common room in the retirement condo building was decked out with a large Christmas tree that had presents underneath it. There was a big stage at one end and the walls were trimmed with garland, and someone had gotten a little crazy with the mistletoe, which had been hung nearly every five feet.

The cookies and punch were on tables along one wall. Dante had set up an Inferno Brewing bar at the back and there were rows of chairs that were filled with residents from the building, family members of the kids that had come and other invited guests.

Mrs. B and her group took the stage, along with a group of children between six to fourteen, and they started their show with a rendition of Elton John's "Step into Christmas." Paisley stood out of the way, very aware that she was pregnant and feeling like she wanted to build some sort of tradition for her child. The child that she'd kept from Sean because she wasn't sure of the man he was. But as she watched him as Candace coaxed him up to sing along with them as they moved into a jazzy rendition of "The Twelve Days of Christmas," she realized that she was starting to like him more.

It was clear to her that Sean sort of came alive when he had an audience, and it was interesting to watch as he sang along with the women and kids. God, he was so hot when he sang. If she took away the fact that he was drop-dead gorgeous, she still wanted him more than she should. She wasn't sure she trusted him and couldn't just let her hormones take her back into his arms, but she wanted to be there.

However, she wasn't making decisions for only herself now; she had the baby to consider.

"So… I really am liking Sean," Olive said as she came up and linked her arm through Paisley's. "I mean, Jack was great, but now that we know who he really is, he seems…less muted."

"I know. It's like I saw him through a frosted window before," she murmured.

"Why don't you sound happier about this?" her friend asked.

"Oh, I am. Sean pointed out that I'd never told him about Mrs. B and I realized there is a big part of me that I've kept from him too."

"Hey, you were getting to know each other. You never said you were Judy or something like that. He knew from the first the woman you are," Olive said, defending her.

"But he wasn't wrong. I do pretend that I'm not my dad's daughter a lot."

Olive hugged her. "I pretend I wasn't a mean girl… You know Dante also doesn't like to look backward, but one thing I learned from him was we are all products of our past. You are the woman you are today because of the man your father was. I am not saying you were right to keep it from Sean, but I think you were getting close to letting him in."

Olive's words offered some comfort. She had been ready to share more with Sean before everything had gone down, but the truth about her father made her ashamed. Growing up a con man's daughter wasn't something she had wanted him to know. But if she wanted total honesty from him, she had to give him the same.

That meant she had to tell him about the baby.

No more pretending that she wasn't sure of the man he was. Today he had stepped up for her. With no thought for what was in it for him. And honestly, she hadn't expected it. Which made her admire him even more.

"Hey, lady, want to join us on stage?" Sean said, coming over to her. He had donned a red Santa cap.

"No. That's not my thing," she said. Something that was her thing was reinforcing the image of her clients. And Sean was one now. "But this is the kind of Christmassy event that would really help your movie. Do you mind if take some photos and videos and then we can share them online later?"

"I don't mind, but we should check with the ladies first. I don't want it to seem I used them for the film," he said.

"I'll talk to Mrs. B. Oh, and thanks for asking Dante to come set up a bar," she murmured. "This is the first year we've had this many of the residents downstairs. I noticed a lot of parents stayed as well."

"It was nothing. I'm glad to see everyone having fun and spreading Christmas cheer." Then he admitted gruffly, "I honestly didn't think I'd like this as much as I am."

"Why not?" she asked.

"I'm not grinchy or anything but Christmas

doesn't really do anything for me. But singing with the ladies and hearing their stories… I'm starting to sort of get it."

She smiled at him as Candace called his name. "I can see that. I think I have some competition in Candace."

He had started to turn, but stopped and put his hand on her shoulder. "She is just a flirt. I want more than that with you."

How much more?

She didn't ask that question out loud. There was still too much unsaid between them, but she had the feeling they were on a path that she hadn't expected. One that she hoped wouldn't end when she told him about the baby.

He leaned down and kissed her, just a quick brush of lips, and then winked and pointed above her head. "Mistletoe."

He headed over to Candace and Paisley just watched him walk away. That kiss had stirred memories and new longings inside of her. But she'd made a promise to herself that if they slept together again it would be with no secrets between them.

She just hadn't expected the person with the secrets to be her.

Sean enjoyed entertaining and singing with Candace and Mrs. B. It was something that he hadn't done in a long time. He realized that a part of him was trying to impress Paisley, but he couldn't do it in his normal manner. And in a way, it was freeing because she wanted to see who he was. She wasn't expecting the Hollywood superstar.

Just the man.

He was starting to realize that maybe he'd spent too long trying to divide his life into compartments. But when some of the parents of the kids recognized him and asked for photos, he felt his guard coming back up and he shifted away from what Paisley needed him to be into the persona where, if he was totally honest, he felt the most comfortable.

He joked with the men, charmed the women and did his best to be fun with the kids. The more people who came up to him for photos, the less like Paisley's man he felt.

He couldn't complain and he would never turn away a fan, but he realized that for the first time the spotlight chafed. He wanted to just be here as… *Jack*. But that wasn't who he was. This was his life. He glanced around for Paisley and noticed she was talking to Dante and Olive. He took one last photo and then made his excuses to go join her.

She looked up as he approached, their eyes met and something familiar passed between them. All those months of living together had made them a couple. His heart raced as he realized he didn't want to screw this up. Whatever messed-up mind game he was playing with himself, trying to figure out if he was Jack or Sean or something in between, he wanted the result to be whatever Paisley needed him to be.

The line at the bar had died down as the evening was winding down as well. Olive and Dante were talking quietly and Paisley stepped away from her friends, taking his hand and leading him over to a small anteroom that was being used as a cloakroom during the event.

"Paisley?"

"I just wanted to say thank you again for all you've done. I mean, I wasn't sure what you used your celebrity for but the man I saw tonight…he doesn't seem all that different to Jack."

He shrugged, crossing his arms over his chest to keep from reaching for her. How could he explain to her what he didn't understand himself? "Obviously, Jack is part of who I am. What did you mean by how I would use my celebrity?"

She chewed on her lower lip for a second then shook her head as if coming to some internal decision. "Just how you treated your fans and how natural you were with Mrs. B and Candace. I know you probably don't want to hear this…but I wasn't sure you weren't going to be an asshole."

That elicited a chuckle out of him.

"I do try not to be too douchey around the public," he replied drolly.

"You were way better than that," she said. "Also… what you said earlier, about me not really sharing everything—you were spot on. I don't know why I do that."

But he was pretty sure she did.

"We all try to hide what we perceive as the ugly things in our past," he stated. "I do it too."

"What do you mean *perceive*?" she asked. "I'm not just pretending my dad did those things."

"What I mean is we see them as flaws and bad marks against us, but in reality, your father's criminal activities have made you the woman you are today. It's made you stronger. And all of us have something like that in our past."

"What is it for you?" she asked him quietly.

"Ego. Arrogance. I mean I need both of them to be successful, to have the confidence to believe I can convince an audience I'm someone else. But at the same time, it can create a barrier. It leaves me feeling cold, as if I'm not sure what part of me is real," he said. "I think it did that for you as well."

She shook her head and wrapped her arms around him in a hug. He embraced her back, savoring her warmth as she turned to rest her cheek on his chest "We all feel like we're faking it, Sean. And as much as you were lying about your name and your job, I'm starting to see that you weren't pretending about too much else…unless you are now?"

He wasn't sure how to respond to that. Honestly, with Paisley in his arms he couldn't think straight. Her breasts were pressed against his chest and he was doing his level best not to cup her butt and lift her more fully into his body, then kiss her. Claim the kiss that he'd been craving since he'd walked away from her that night everything went wrong.

But he also didn't want to gloss over what, for him, was a tender moment. He could count on one hand the times that someone had simply hugged him and made him feel cared for the way that Paisley was doing right now.

"I'm not faking it, Paisley. I'll tell you the truth, though. I have no idea what I'm doing and I'm sort of winging it."

She smiled at that admission. "Me too. I want… I want this Christmas to be a new start for us. What do you say?"

"I'd like that too. No more secrets," he promised.

She sort of blinked up at him and then went on her tiptoes to kiss him, and he didn't think any more of it. He just held her close and thanked God he had a second chance with her.

Paisley hadn't realized how much she'd missed being in his arms until this moment. And she knew she'd taken the coward's way out by kissing him, but she wasn't quite ready to tell him about their baby. Which meant she wasn't ready to agree to no more secrets. She really liked what she'd seen of Sean today, but another part of her was still struggling.

This kiss was passionate and familiar, yet with the last few days between them, it felt brand-new as well. His tongue moved over hers and she sucked it deeper into her mouth. She lifted one arm to wrap around his shoulders and pushed her fingers into the thick hair at the back of his neck. Everything about him was different but the same, she thought.

It was like stating something new and this time... she didn't want to screw it up.

The door opened behind them and she stepped back with Sean's arm staying around her shoulders.

"Sorry to interrupt, kids," Candace said. "But folks are getting ready to leave. You want to come say goodbye while they collect their coats?"

"Of course. We were just—" Paisley began.

"I'm old but I still haven't forgotten what it's like to be with my man," the elderly woman said with a wink.

Sean shook his head, laughing as they followed her out of the anteroom and into the main room, where kids and parents were waiting to collect their coats. He signed a few more autographs and Paisley used that moment as a chance to step away. She was losing her resolve. She wanted to just curl into his arms and pretend she could forget about her pregnancy and her past. But she couldn't.

She needed a distraction and turned, as she always did, to her work. She used the high-quality camera on her phone to film Sean talking to the kids. He really had a way of being whatever was needed in a situation.

That niggled. But did it niggle enough to justify

keeping the baby a secret? He said he wanted to start over.

No secrets.

She was reaching, trying to justify her silence. Then she remembered something her mother had said when they'd been going through her father's public trial. That they didn't owe anyone explanations. She said each of them had to figure out how to live in the shadow of what he'd done.

Paisley sighed. She had to figure out how to live with this baby and if she wanted to tell Sean. He was still thinking he wanted to get to know the woman he'd deceived…but was she being too hard on him? She wasn't sure if she wasn't trying to reach for anger to make herself feel better about her silence.

Sean glanced over at her and must have sensed the trepidation on her face because he quirked an eyebrow at her. She forced a smile and shook her head, pointing to her phone.

God. What was she doing?

It seemed like she was compulsively deceiving him. She turned away and walked into the public restroom off the lobby, and went into one of the stalls. She just stood there for a minute. One way or another, she had to stop this.

No secrets was what he'd asked for from her. She had to either fess up that she was still keeping one, or tell him she needed time before she could share. But the truth was she had already been half in love with

Jack when she'd realized he was Sean. She wanted this second chance to find out if he was the man she'd thought he was.

And there was no second chance if she was lying.

She knew that. She wasn't about to mess this up. Sean was trying and she had to at least meet him halfway.

"Hey, Pais, you in here?" Olive called.

Guiltily, she flushed the toilet so her friend wouldn't realize she'd been simply hiding and then she came out. "Hey. What's up?"

Olive tipped her head to the side, studying her closely. "Just checking on you. Sean said you looked like something was up."

"Just the same something that I've been dealing with," Paisley admitted. She touched her stomach so that the other woman would know without her having to say anything. She didn't want to risk anyone overhearing she was pregnant before she had the chance to tell Sean.

"Oh, did today help at all?" Olive asked. "I know it's still a lot to take in with the Jack-Sean thing and…*that*."

Paisley wasn't sure if it had helped or not, but she knew she didn't want to talk about it with Olive. She wasn't sure how she felt and didn't want to stay something that she'd later regret. "Maybe. I mean Sean was great today, wasn't he?"

"He was better than great!" Olive exclaimed. "For my two cents, I don't think he was faking it."

"I don't, either," Paisley admitted. "He said…no more secrets."

Olive's eyes widened. "That's great, but you still have one."

"Yeah, and I don't want to rush telling him or deceive him but… I don't know what to do," she said.

"It's okay to not know," Olive reassured her. "I think whatever you decide he'll understand."

"Really?"

"No," Olive admitted. "I was just trying to be a good friend. I mean, I know you can't say anything, but he's going to be hurt that you didn't and I don't think you should rush it. But he's a man so I don't know if he'll get the subtlety of you waiting, the way I do."

Paisley laughed and nodded. "Exactly. I'm trapped and I have no idea how I'm going to get out."

"You'll figure it out—you always do," Olive said as they left the bathroom to find the room had emptied significantly and only Dante and Sean were waiting. Olive hugged her and they said goodbye. Paisley waved to Dante and as she turned to face Sean, she felt butterflies in her stomach and her heart pounding too loudly.

No more secrets was what he wanted and she had to find a way to honor that and to keep her pregnancy to herself until she was ready.

"It's started snowing... Want to walk for a bit?" he asked.

"Yes. I love snow."

"You told me that," he said. "I'm a remembering kind of man."

Eight

Paisley pulled up the collar of her coat around her neck as they left Mrs. B's condo building and started to walk toward Michigan Avenue. She thought about last Christmas and how she'd wished her life would be in a different place this year. Well, that wish had come true, but dang, she'd had no idea *how* different her life would become. She'd had an affair with a movie star, was pregnant and her best friends were both in committed relationships.

She started to laugh and Sean turned to her, snow sticking to his thick eyelashes and the skullcap he was wearing.

"What?"

"Just thinking how surprising life can be," she murmured.

"Yeah? What in particular?"

She shrugged. "Well, turns out I had an affair with a megastar. Didn't see that coming."

"If you'd known from the start, would it have changed things?"

"Heck yeah. I wouldn't have flirted with Sean O'Neill. I mean I'm not exactly in your orbit. It would have felt weird."

"Fame isn't real. You know that, right?" he asked her.

"Yeah, of course. It's so surreal—how do you live with it and stay normal?"

"Well, you know I have a big ego," he answered with a wink.

"Except you don't, not really."

"Well, I know I'm good at my craft," he said. "The photographers and gossip sites that always talk about me, they aren't exactly my favorites. We would have never known each other…"

She nodded. "I see the point you're making. If you hadn't lied we would never have gotten together. And you're right."

"Ah…finally got you to admit I'm right and I can't help but feel that I'm still wrong," he said.

"I didn't mean it that way."

He stopped walking and put his hand on her arm, and she turned toward him. The snow was still so light that it just fell in random flakes on both of them.

This was the kind of picture-perfect moment that she had would have expected from a Sean O'Neill movie. Paisley knew that she was trying to make him into the superstar, but it was too late. Because she already knew the man behind the fame. She was just afraid to trust that man. Afraid that it might be just one more role from the award-winning actor.

"I know. It's just…the more we discuss it the more I realize that lying was the only option I had, and yet it's the one reason why you can't trust me. I mean, there's no other way I could have actually gotten to know you." He blew out a breath. "I want to say the right thing, but let's be honest, I'm not a writer. I just bring someone else's words to life."

She shook her head again, reaching up to touch his cheek because he looked so…alone. "You are doing okay. None of us really know the right thing to say. We can't edit the dumb stuff that we blurt out… I know I wish I could. And…well, I'm trying to let it go. As you pointed out, I was hiding things too."

"Some parts of ourselves are harder to share. I don't know about your past relationships, but when I'm dating I tend to try to be the best version of myself," he said.

"Yeah, me too. I never lead with 'my dad's a felon.'"

He laughed, as she'd hoped he would, then took her hand in his, pulled her close and claimed another kiss. She sighed when their lips met and her tongue brushed over his as her fingers tangled in the hair at the back of his neck.

She wrapped her arms around his chest this time and he lifted her off her feet so that her body was pressed to his.

"That kiss…" she said when he put her on her feet.

"Good?"

"Not bad maybe a little more practice later tonight…"

He threw back his head and laughed, and for the first time since that paparazzo had turned their lives upside down, Paisley felt a real sense of joy sparking between them.

They started walking again toward the lights of Michigan Avenue. She realized that this was how they were starting over. There was no easy way to erase the lies between them, but he was slowly showing her the man he was.

It was another layer to the already complex emotions that she had toward him. She knew better than to dwell on this budding relationship. Because right here, right now, she wanted to be in the moment, but she'd always been a chronic planner. Always trying to find the way to safely get to the next thing, and relationships didn't work that way.

Especially when a baby was involved. Her stomach clenched. How in the world was she going to raise a child? Would she be a good parent to this baby she was carrying? There was no way to plan for this.

"You okay?"

"Um…no. I'm not really. I know you said no more secrets, but I'm not sure I can just tell you everyone of—"

He put a finger to her lips. She nipped at it. "You don't have to. Sometimes honesty means just keeping it real with yourself. When you trust me, you won't be worried about your most personal thoughts."

Was that it?

Was it trust that was keeping her from telling him about the baby? Hell, yes, it was. But also a million other things. Like, would they be a family? Would they try to raise the child together? Or live separate lives and co-parent? Would he even *want* to be a father?

"Paisley, no pressure. Let's just enjoy getting to know each other. We are starting over because we know that we like each other, have wicked chemistry and maybe don't want to walk away, right?"

No pressure? Could she really let all this go…at least for now?

Come on, Paisley, be Elsa from Frozen and let it go. Be the woman in this beautifully snowy December evening with the super hot Hollywood heartthrob.

He started laughing, pulled her into his arms and hugged her. Then, using his hand, he tipped back her head so that their eyes met. "Lady, you are trying too hard. Just be."

"Ugh. You know I can't—"

She broke off as his mouth came down on hers

with a fierceness she wasn't expecting. The spark that had always happened between them sprang to life and she closed her eyes, felt her fears and worries start to ebb away. There was no room for them in her head when Sean kissed her like this.

His mouth moved over hers with a familiarity and sureness as she tipped her head to the side and returned the embrace. Rubbed her tongue over his and deeper into his mouth. She couldn't help but feel that something that had been lost was sort of found again.

Sean knew there was no easy way to win trust. Or to just trust and be himself. He had understood that she was scared. His celebrity did that. There was no way that most people in their daily lives ever thought he could be just like them. But he realized that he didn't really care what anyone else thought. It was just Paisley.

Having her back in his arms like this made something hard and cold in his stomach start to melt. He was on fire for her. His cock hardened, and he shifted his hips so that his erection didn't brush against her because he didn't want her to think this was only about sex for him. He'd hadn't acknowledged even to himself that he was afraid he'd lost her for good. He refused to allow any more thoughts in his head. He had her in his arms and he didn't plan to let her go. Her mouth tasted as good as he remembered. More exotic and addictive than anything he'd eaten or any drug he'd taken. He wanted her.

He wanted to get back into her bed, not just because she drove him wild with desire, but so that that tense thing inside of him could relax and maybe he could convince himself he was still the man she wanted. He was working hard to get her back, but in his mind was that same fear that had always driven him. That he wasn't good enough. That he'd never get her back. That this was the last time he'd hold her.

She didn't trust him.

That was huge. He knew it. Could he use their physical bond to build trust? God, he hoped so.

He heard people coming toward them and lifted his head, keeping her tucked to his side. "Let's go."

"Where?"

"Look at the windows. There is one I think you will like," he said. He'd noticed it recently when he'd been out running errands. He and Paisley hadn't really talked about Christmas, but she had a print on her wall. A Norman Rockwell one that showed a little girl in front of a fireplace decked in garland with a tree next to it.

He'd seen a version of it with a group of children standing by the fireplace and he hoped she'd like it. He wanted to show her that even though he hadn't been truthful about everything, he'd been committed to her. That he'd been real with her. *Seen* her.

"Can you do that? Won't people recognize you?" she asked.

"Nah. I mean some might, but when I'm with you, wearing a beanie, I think we can be unobtrusive."

"Okay. Then sure… I'd love that." She slipped her gloved hand into his and they laced their fingers together. He took a deep breath, realizing that he hadn't expected this. The kiss must have softened her more than he'd expected.

Michigan Avenue was busy with foot traffic and Christmas music spilled out of the doors of shops as they opened. He kept Paisley close to his side as they moved through the crowds until they got to the window he'd noticed previously. Then he pulled her to a stop in front of it.

"This one," he said, stepping behind her and putting his arms around her. He heard her breath catch and she turned her head to the side and up, to look back at him.

"How'd you know I love this scene?"

"You have a print of it," he said.

"It's tiny…like postcard-size! I didn't think you'd notice."

"I noticed."

She turned away from the window, winding her arms around his waist. "What else did you notice?"

"That you always open the blind as soon as you wake up and stand and look at the sky. And that you wake up early but don't want to talk for twenty minutes," he said. He'd learned that the *hard* way.

She laughed. "True. I noticed that you wake up early and exercise. Always fifty push-ups and then one hundred crunches."

He arched one eyebrow at her. "Well, if I don't

start moving then I start thinking and... I don't always like where my mind goes."

Especially when he'd been deceiving her. It was hard to stay positive when he knew that he wasn't being honest, so he had to move to keep himself in the right headspace. But he didn't want to tell her that.

"I journal when I get like that. I guess pretending to be someone else was stressful," she said.

He put his arm around her and turned her away from the window to start them walking again. "It isn't being someone else, it was not telling you that was adding to my stress levels."

She tipped her head to the side. "I think we all have stressors. My dad couldn't help himself when he saw someone who trusted too easily... He had to see how far he could take it."

"What about you?" He noticed that she tended to bring her dad into the conversation when she didn't want to share too much.

"I make lists. Like right now, I'm making one with pros and cons."

"You are?" He lifted an eyebrow. "What are you trying not to stress over?"

"Inviting you back into my apartment. That kiss earlier was pretty good," she said.

"Again, the faint praise."

"I thought we agreed you didn't need your ego stroked," she teased.

"Did we? I'd never turn down being stroked by you."

She ran her finger down the side of his jaw. "You wouldn't? So that was real?"

"Everything between you and I was real, Pais," he admitted gruffly.

They reached the end of the main shopping area on Michigan Avenue and she slanted a glance his way. "Was it? I feel like pretending I don't want you back in my bed is a kind of lie I'm telling myself for the sake of my pride."

Pride. Until she mentioned it, he'd been happily ignoring the fact that he might be here simply for his pride. That the reason he couldn't just let her walk away was that every woman wanted him. Well, not every woman…but quite a damn few, and there was something about Paisley maybe not wanting him just because he was Sean O'Neill.

He was distracting himself—anything to keep from breaking down and begging her to take him back. Not that he'd beg…but he wanted her back in his bed because she was a hot, sensual woman. There was something inside of him that was convinced that if he got her back there, he'd be able to convince her that she belonged with him.

"You're being surprisingly quiet," she said. "Do you not want me?"

"I want you too damn much, lady. But this has to be your decision."

"I think I'd rather it was ours."

Ours.

Something shifted inside of him, which he ignored. He wasn't going to assess why being part of a couple with her was resonating so deeply inside him. Not now.

She gave him that sweet, intimate smile that she only used with him, and as much as he wanted to pretend that it didn't affect him, he sort of unraveled inside. He pulled her back into his arms, because not touching, not holding her, wasn't working. He *needed* her in his arms. She hugged him and tipped back her head as he brought his down toward hers, kissing her long and deep. And when he lifted his head, he knew they needed to go somewhere private.

She had always had this effect on him. She turned him on like no other woman. So quickly, like a marshmallow melting in a mug of hot chocolate. She made his walls crumble until all he wanted was to be in her and with her.

"Yes. Let's go back to your place."

She nodded, chewing her lower lip as she used her phone to order an Uber for them. They only had to wait a few minutes before they were picked up. She didn't say anything and neither did he—they both just sat close to each other watching the buildings pass as the driver took them to her apartment building. He dropped them off and Sean remembered the last time he'd been in her apartment, and hesitated.

He'd hadn't been back since the morning he'd left

to get his hair dyed back to his natural color and shaved off his beard to lose the last vestiges of Jack.

He thought that Paisley might be thinking about it too. She hesitated at the outer door and he wondered if she'd changed her mind.

"You still want to do this?"

"Yes… I was just thinking about…the last time."

"Me too. That morning when you were harried and had to get to work, and I was lazing around because we'd wrapped filming and I knew I had to tell you who I was."

"Yeah…what was that like?" she asked.

"Scary."

"Ha, you're not scared of anything," she said.

He shook his head. If only she knew how much she scared him on a soul-deep level. He couldn't figure her out. And normally, he was good at figuring out what made people tick, what they wanted or needed from him, but Paisley was still a mystery.

"Maybe not like jump scare but there are other fears," he told her.

She sort of wrapped one arm around her stomach and then reached out with her free hand to unlock the outer door and lead him into the building. "I know about those. You just sort of ooze confidence, even when I thought your job was sort of dead-end, I still felt it."

He laughed at that statement. "I do have confidence—some would say arrogance, but that doesn't negate fear. One of my mentors when I first started said the bigger he got, the more he felt he had to lose, and the fear grew along with his career."

Her apartment was on the third floor and Paisley always took the stairs. He hadn't realized that he'd led them to the stairwell until they were both walking up. There was something so familiar about this. None of those first-date jitters or anything like that. He realized that his fears weren't strong when she was by his side. It was when he was alone…as it always had been.

"I can see that. You have more at stake and more to lose," she said. "It's different for us at IDG because it's not just me. I have Olive and Delaney with me. If one of us gets scared then the other two talk her down."

He could see that. Her friendship with the other two women was a big part of Paisley. They grounded her in her life and in her career, and he envied her that, he realized. It must have been nice to always have someone to lean on. He had been slowly letting Bert into his life but Sean was always careful to remember the other man worked for him.

He held open the door to the third floor and Paisley walked into the hallway toward her apartment. "Is it weird for you coming back here?"

"Yes and no," he said. He almost told her that it felt like he was coming home but he stopped himself. He didn't want to reveal that this small apartment of hers in Chicago had felt more like his home than his mansion in Malibu.

She unlocked her front door and turned to look up at him. The expression in her gaze was serious. "When you left, did you plan to never come back here?"

"No."

Paisley just continued looking at him. She wanted more. And he wasn't sure how to put it into words. "I think I had deluded myself into believing that once you knew who I really was, you'd sort of laugh it off and we'd keep having our affair."

"But I didn't."

"No, you didn't. But I'm glad you gave me this second chance to start over with no secrets between us."

Nine

Paisley wasn't sure what she'd expected when she brought Sean back to her apartment. Maybe somehow seeing him here would make her realize something she'd missed earlier? Like right now, she just wanted to shove him against the coat closet and kiss him like they used to do. Push his coat off his shoulders and free his cock, and have crazy, hot, hallway sex. Like the very first time…but this wasn't the first time. She stood there watching him, very aware of what his naked body looked like and how good he felt inside of her, but at the same time, her emotions were roiling. Like a blizzard threatening to keep Santa from coming on Christmas Eve.

She wished—*really* wished with her whole damn

heart—that she was one of those people who could just shut off their mind, but she wasn't.

"What are you thinking?"

"About having sex with you against the coat closet."

His pupils dilated and she glanced down to see his dick harden against the front of his jeans. He sort of flushed and tilted his head to the side, then raised both eyebrows at her. "I wouldn't say no."

She shook her head.

"Are *you* saying no?"

"I don't know," she admitted softly. "I'm trying to figure out how to hook up with a guy for the first time when it's not."

"Aw, Paisley, every time with you is like the first time," he said.

"How do you figure?"

He shrugged out of his jacket and let it drop to the floor as he walked toward her. "Every minute with you I'm learning something new. Each layer that you peel away shows me another layer of the woman I thought I knew. And when we make love, I feel like I'm getting deeper and deeper into you."

She blinked at him as he kept coming toward her. Her heart was starting to beat faster, her skin felt hotter and her breasts grew fuller, as they always did when she thought of him. He stopped when there wasn't more than an inch of space between the two of them. She smelled the minty freshness of his breath, the faint fragrance of his aftershave and something else that she associated only with him.

Their eyes met and she knew he wanted her, but he was waiting. Letting her set the pace tonight. She appreciated that, but she didn't know if she could take the lead. She was too aware of her secret, and how she was going to have to tell him about the baby. How would he feel when heard?

"Kiss me," she said.

"With pleasure," he murmured, rubbing his thumb along her bottom lip and she opened her mouth to bite it as shivers spread down her body.

Unable to wait a moment longer, she put her hands on his shoulders and raised herself up on her toes, until their noses brushed and she was staring into his beautiful blue eyes. She wrapped her legs around his hips. His mouth on hers was just as familiar as it had been earlier, but this time the kiss tasted sweeter. This wasn't a do-we-still-like-each-other? embrace. It was one that wasn't meant to end until they were both naked.

Paisley reveled in the feel of his tongue rubbing over hers and his big, warm hands sliding down her back, cupping her butt, as he intensified the kiss. She felt the wall behind her and then he planted one hand against it, pulling off her beanie and watching as her hair tumbled around her face and shoulders.

She broke the kiss. She saw something on his face that she'd never noticed before, and she wanted to explore it. But then all thoughts abandoned her as he put her on her feet and undid the buttons to her coat. She felt the backs of his fingers brushing against her breasts as he undid the buttons and he pushed the coat off her shoulders to the floor.

She was so hot for him. It was all she could do not to rip her sweater over her head, then shove off her leggings. But she knew she wanted more than that. More than a quick coupling in the hallway.

She wanted to make love to Sean. To know him the way she'd known Jack and maybe even more.

Sean was done debating about everything. He was back in Paisley's apartment—she wanted him back in her arms and that was enough for him. Her coat fell to the floor near his and, honestly, he wanted her hot, quick and against the coat closet in the foyer of her apartment.

But this was their first time with no lies between them and a part of him wanted to do it right. But he knew there was no thinking. From the moment she'd said she was thinking about sex against the wall, he had barely been able to hold on to his control. His mind had gone into mating mode. There was no other way to describe it. His hands were shaking a bit as he tried to go slowly and not just rip off her clothes and get inside of her as fast as he could.

This was Paisley.

The one woman he wanted more than all the others.

The one woman that he was trying to win back.

Her hands were on the hem of the sweater vest he was wearing and he felt her drawing it up over his head. He impatiently yanked it off himself, then tossed it aside. Her fingers moved to the buttons of his shirt as he reached for her sweater tunic and pulled it up and over her head. He stepped back away from her touch and took a moment to admire her body. The body he had lost the right to see naked when she'd learned he'd been lying to her.

He hadn't thought he'd feel this emotion… What was it exactly? Maybe gratitude, maybe relief. It was tinged with joy and lust. But those two emotions were always prevalent when he was close to her. Sometimes just seeing her smile could make him hard.

She had on a red lacy bra and he reached out to cup one breast, rubbing the palm of his hand over the lacy cup, feeling her nipple harden. Her skin was pale and creamy. He traced his finger around the outline of the cup, teasing himself when what he wanted was to remove that damn bra. But now that he knew she wasn't going to kick him out, he wanted to draw out the anticipation.

This felt…well, like something he couldn't take for granted. She'd left him once and he knew himself too well to think that he wouldn't screw up again and maybe lose her permanently.

He wanted this moment to be one to remember. She put her hands on her hips, which forced her shoulders back and her breasts forward. "Have you suddenly decided you don't want to see me naked?"

"Hell, no. I'm just trying not to push your pants down and take you fast and hard. I want this…ah, hell, this sounds stupid out loud," he said, drawing his hand back and thrusting it through his hair.

She brushed aside his hand and tousled his hair. "Not silly at all. I want this to be special too."

It loosened some of the tension he was carrying, knowing she felt the same as he did about tonight.

Sean pulled her into his arms and kissed her, as he caressed her back and undid her bra strap with one hand. He felt her hands between them, undoing the buttons of his shirt, and then her fingers moved over his chest, her nails lightly scoring his skin, making his cock even harder.

He lifted his head and yanked off her bra, tossing it aside, and then pulled her bare chest against his and held her. Felt the perkiness of her nipples and the curve of her waist as he reached lower, cupping her butt and pulling her more fully into him.

She wrapped her arms around him and rested her head over his heart. Then he felt her turn her head to kiss his pectoral and watched as she looked up at him. Her big blue-gray eyes were full of tears.

"What's wrong?"

"Nothing's wrong. I just didn't think we'd be this close again," she whispered.

He hadn't, either, but he knew that if they started talking, he would more than likely say the wrong thing. So he just lifted her into his arms and strode with her into her bedroom. The layout was familiar, but he noticed that the bedding had been changed and that the bed itself had been moved to the opposite wall.

It pained him to see the proof of how she'd tried to erase him from her life. But he wasn't going away that easily. Tonight he'd learned so much about this woman and realized he still had so much more to discover. But there were three things he knew with one-hundred-percent certainty... He liked her. He wanted her. And he wasn't going to let her go.

Sean set her on her feet next to the bed. He shrugged out of his shirt as he toed off his shoes and then his hands went to his pants. But hers were there first, undoing his belt.

He reached for the waistband of her leggings and pushed his hands underneath the layers of both the leggings and her underwear, sliding them down her legs. They got caught on her boots and he bent down to unzip the boots and remove them for her.

His eyes roved up her naked body as she stepped out of the leggings and panties. Sean's breath caught in his throat and his cock got harder. This woman was *his*.

He didn't know why he hadn't realize it earlier. Or how he'd let himself get distracted by pride, but he wanted her and he wasn't about to let her go.

Not tonight and not ever. And now that there

weren't any lies left between them, there was no reason for him to let her go.

Paisley shoved aside the embarrassment she felt when he saw the way she'd moved the bed and other furniture around in the room. She'd gone to Saks and bought all new bedding as well, trying to erase him from her apartment in a way that she hadn't been able to erase him from her thoughts.

She wondered why she wasn't having second thoughts now. Why was she just standing here naked in his arms, reaching for the zipper of his pants and trying to get him inside her, instead of pushing him away? This could go so badly.

But…

It could also go *so right*. And she remembered how right it had felt when she'd been in his arms. And in her dream life, how right she hoped it could be with the two of them before their baby was born.

Her conscience gave her a huge shove.

Tell him about the baby, it said.

But she ignored it as she started to shove his pants down his legs. He brushed aside her hands and chucked them off himself, before pulling her into his arms and kissing her again. She felt him push her backward with his arms still around her and his mouth on hers. The strength of his iron embrace kept her close until she felt the bed at her back and he came down over her, positioning himself between her legs.

She looked up into his face and she almost started to cry. She had missed him. It hadn't even been that long but she'd missed *this*. She closed her eyes and turned her face away, but felt his thumbs against her temples wiping away the tears that had slipped out.

He didn't say anything but she felt his mouth against her neck and then it drifted slowly lower as he kissed her shoulders and the curve of her breast. His lips closed over her nipple, suckling her into his mouth, and her feminine center clenched and she felt herself go liquid. She reached between their bodies for his cock, stroking him and trying to direct him to her pussy.

She wanted him inside her. Enough waiting and trying to make this first time back together into something different. It was…and yet it wasn't.

This man had made love to her before and had left a mark on her soul and a child in her body. He'd changed her even if he didn't know it and having sex with him again was her chance…to just reclaim some of what she'd lost when she'd found out he'd lied.

She wasn't doing this for revenge or any other reason than she'd truly missed him. Missed the way his face softened when he looked at her and how he smiled in that intimate way that was reserved only for her when they were alone like this. She opened her eyes, reaching up to cup his face in her hands. Warmth flowed through her as she felt the stubble of his beard coming through and she rubbed her thumb over his jawline.

"I've missed this."

"Me too," he rasped as he moved his hips until she felt the tip of his erection at her entrance. She planted her feet on the bed and lifted her hips to urge him inside of her, but he didn't thrust forward.

"I'm—"

"No more talking. Just action," she said.

If he said anything else she was going to have to tell him about the baby. Heck, she probably should have already told him but she was afraid.

He smiled and leaned down to suckle her nipple as he drove himself deep inside her, and not a moment too soon. She stopped thinking about the consequences of keeping silent and just let herself be filled with him, feeling him thrusting into her, and she arched her back to try to take more of him.

She wanted him deeper and harder, and urged him on with whispered demands. He met them. Cupping her butt in his hands to tip up her hips and pounding himself into her again and again until she felt her body start to climax. She cried out his name as she did and he shifted to lift her legs higher as he drove into her at a frantic pace and then he was grunting her name as he came inside of her.

He collapsed against her, his head resting on her chest, his breath brushing over her skin. Basking in their closeness, she put her arms around his shoulders, running her fingers through his hair. And as she held him to her, she knew that whatever other lies she'd been telling herself, she could no longer pretend that she didn't want Sean in her and the baby's lives. She closed her eyes and the image of a family that had always sort of eluded her in real life was there.

A family with her and Sean, and the unborn child inside of her.

Paisley licked her lips and fear gripped her hard. She wondered if this was at all how Sean had felt when he knew he had to tell her the truth of his identity. Had he been wracked with guilt and fear or...?

"Were you afraid to lose me?" she asked quietly.

He shifted around, disconnecting their bodies and propping his weight on his elbows as he looked down at her. She saw a brief sort of panicked expression go over his face and then she thought she saw him slip into another character. Not his real self, but someone he thought she wanted him to be.

"No—"

"I thought you said no more secrets."

He sighed. "I don't want to fuck this up."

"And telling me the truth will?" she asked.

"No, but I might not say the right thing."

She reached up to caress his cheek. "Just be you—that's the right thing."

Ten

Be himself. He was always better as one of the leading men he'd played over his lifetime. But Sean had the feeling that anything less than the truth wasn't going to sit well with either one of them.

"Okay, so…"

It was harder than he expected. He could be blunt and just say that he hadn't really thought about it. Certainly not after sex. He was tired and wanted to wash up, pull her into his arms and go to sleep.

She quirked an eyebrow, prompting him to continue. "So…"

"I didn't think about it when we were in bed. I'm pretty much thinking about how you look naked, how good you feel in my arms and how soon can I have you again," he said. He bent down to kiss her belly because he didn't want to look at her expression. The room smelled of Christmas potpourri and sex.

He didn't hate it.

"That's what you think about when we make love?"

"I wouldn't exactly say there's much thinking going on when you are naked and next to me," he admitted sardonically.

She laughed. "I guess that makes sense."

He shifted around until he was lying at the head of the bed and pulled her up into his arms, then tucked the corner of the comforter over them. "What's going through your head, Pais?"

She snuggled closer to him, her hand drawing random patterns in the light dusting of hair on his chest. "The usual stuff. The sex was great, I really like this guy, did I clear my inbox at work, I wonder if he wants a drink—"

"Stop. That's too much for one person to be thinking."

"I can't. My mind is always going," she said. "But I'm curious how you felt about the secret of your true identity. Did it worry you ever?"

He took a deep breath. She had questions and he wanted to answer them. "Still okay if I just be myself?"

She shifted around, using her hand to brace herself. "Yes, always. Just be Sean."

"Well, I thought about it when you were worrying about my job prospects. When you kept trying in your quiet way to encourage me to dream bigger. And I knew that my Jack persona wasn't measuring up in a way that Sean could."

She chewed her lower lip, furrowing her brow as she put her head back on his shoulder. "Sorry about that. I guess maybe I saw something more in you."

He rubbed his hand up and down her back and then hugged her to him. "I liked it. You were supportive of me even though it seemed I liked working at that run-down gym. One thing that struck me about you, Pais, was the way you didn't judge. You might have thought I could do better but not because you were embarrassed to be with me. Just that you thought I'd be happier if I was."

He could tell she was smiling because he felt her cheek move against him. "I was *never* embarrassed by you. I hate that there is so much worth tied to occupation in society. I mean, as long as you could pay your bills and seem content, there's nothing else to judge…" She hesitated. "Well, if I'm being totally honest, when I briefly thought you might be a criminal… I didn't love that."

She wouldn't. She was honest to her core. He wished he could have been.

"So anything else you want to know?"

"When are you going back the West Coast?" she asked.

Sean grimaced. Truthfully, he hadn't really considered it. He had a script to look at that his agent had sent him and was going to have to do press for the movie he'd wrapped on. But he wanted to resolve this relationship with Paisley first. Needed to know if this was just a Christmas affair or something that would last longer.

"That depends."

She shifted around and shook her head as she looked down at him. "I hate that. Just say it."

"Well, I'm not the only person in this relationship and so my decision depends on you. If you kick me out and say 'thanks for the sex, be seeing you,' then I guess there's no reason to stay."

"Fair enough," she said. "For the record, I'll never say *be seeing you*."

"You won't?"

"No."

He arched one eyebrow at her.

"I'd say…hit the road, Jack."

He laughed, realizing she was done talking about the past and wanted to move back to the present. "Indeed. So other than the new bedroom, what else have you done to the place in the week I've been gone."

She flushed. "Not much. I'm going to start decorating for Christmas, but my brother hasn't had time to come and help me put up the tree."

"Was Christmas good growing up?" he asked, thinking of her dad and her family situation.

She shrugged. "Yeah. I thought…well, it doesn't matter. But Dad always made sure Christmas morning was picture-perfect."

"I've got a love-hate relationship with the season. Some years I'm all in, and I hire a team to deck out my Malibu mansion, and other years I order a case of scotch and sit in my den alone."

"You're a man of extremes?"

He didn't think he was, but truthfully, he had always been sort of up and down with holidays. "The thing is Christmas is about family, and when yours isn't great…sometimes the best you can do is get through it."

She hugged him. "Let's do Christmas together."

Instead of answering, he pulled her into his arms.

He wasn't pinning much on celebrating the holidays with her, but for the first time he was thinking about December 25th and it wasn't with total dread. He knew that had more than a little to do with Paisley.

He moved above her, growling deep in his throat as her hands went to his cock, and then he felt her mouth roam over his chest.

Her tongue darted out and brushed against his nipple. He arched as he put his hand on the back of her head, urging her to stay where she was.

As he moved his hands lower, caressing her between her legs, he shifted around so that she could straddle him. Their eyes met as she sank slowly down on his erection.

She rode him and he held off his orgasm as long as he could until he felt her pussy tighten around him, and she threw her back and called out his name as she came. Then, clutching her tighter, he thrust into her until he emptied himself. He held her in his arms after. She was quiet and drifted to sleep but his mind was active.

He had a second chance with Paisley and he didn't want to fuck it up.

Doing Christmas together. Well, it was what she wanted. She had picture in her head of what the holiday should be. And if she were being totally honest, there had been a few Christmases when she'd been a child that had been okay. But the truth was more often than not it hadn't been. It had given her a lot of time to dream of what the holiday should be.

And that was a big ask to put on herself and on Sean. But the next morning, when he suggested they drive to a Christmas-tree lot outside the city and pick a tree out together…well, he was already checking off boxes.

He'd gone back to his hotel to get changed and she'd put on her red and green plaid cigarette pants and a bold sweater. She'd been nauseous this morning, but luckily, she'd been able to hide it by dashing to the bathroom while he'd been preparing bagels for them. And she'd been glad when he'd left, because she could lie down for a few minutes.

It was well past time to tell him about the baby. At this point, she couldn't even say what she was waiting for.

After last night, she had no excuse.

They were closer now than they'd ever been, after making love several times throughout the night. She hadn't realized how much she'd missed having his arms around her until he was back in her bed. She hoped that this was real, but if growing up with her con-man father had taught her anything it was that everyone could be fooled.

She'd let herself be fooled by Sean once, and honestly, she still wasn't entirely sure why he was hanging around. Unless he was falling for her too…right?

That could be the only real reason.

But she was so used to being let down it was hard to believe that. It had hurt really bad when she'd learned the truth that Jack was really Sean, but part of her hadn't been surprised. He'd been too good to be true.

And now, was it just more of the same?

Or could she take him at his word. Trust that what he'd said was the truth. They'd agreed to do Christmas together. She wanted that more than she would admit to him, but she had always felt like sort of an outsider at the holidays. Olive was close to her family, and while Delaney had a love-hate relationship with her father and wealthy relatives, she always went to their many parties and get-togethers.

Whereas Paisley got together with her brother and sister if they had time and sometimes her mom. They just weren't that close. She touched her stomach as she waited for Sean to return. She wanted what Olive had with her family for this unborn child. She realized she wanted it for herself too.

She thought Sean might need it as well. He'd always been alone; he'd admitted it to her. Maybe this baby was fate's gift to them.

The doorbell rang and she shook her head as she grabbed her coat and went to answer it.

"Hello, gorgeous," Sean said.

"Hiya, handsome."

He pulled her into his arms and kissed her, long and slow and deep. As if he had all the time in the world. She wrapped herself around him and kissed him back.

Then she stepped out of the house, determined to leave her negative thoughts behind and enjoy this morning out with Sean. "You got ready quickly."

"I didn't want to waste time away from you," he said. "I rented an SUV. Ready?"

"I am," she confirmed. Before she knew it, they were in his rental and on their way out of the city. He had a Christmas playlist providing music for their drive and she noticed most of the songs were traditional.

"It's funny that for a guy who's got a sort of unconventional Christmas movie out, you really like classics," she said.

He glanced over at her and then quickly back to the road. "It just felt like a traditional playlist was needed for this outing."

"I like it. So you made this for me?"

He shrugged. "For *us*. I mean I've never gotten a Christmas tree before. I've had them and all that, but someone else always put them up and they were just sort of there. I never really did anything like this."

She reached over to touch his thigh, squeezing the hard muscle. There was so much about Sean's seemingly charmed life that was less than spectacular. "I've decorated a lot of things. Sometimes trees, sometimes a rubber plant—whatever we could find."

"I'd have thought Christmas with a con man—"

"That could be your next movie," she interrupted.

"Ha." He glanced over at her again. "Don't want to talk about that?"

She looked out at the passing landscape on the edge of the interstate. All the pretty little neighborhoods. "It's not that. I mean, some years we had the best and brightest Christmas, all the presents and a huge tree, but sometimes we'd have to leave it all behind the next day to get out of town or stuff like that. Other years we'd be in a motel in Florida decorating the potted plant in the corner. Christmas has always been…more of a letdown than anything else."

He reached over and took her hand in his, brushing a kiss across her knuckles. "That's why we need this classic Christmas mix. This year we are going to do it right with each other."

"What is right?" she asked because she'd been wondering that herself.

"Whatever we want. Like this tree—we'll get it and then do you have ornaments?"

"I have some. We can stop and get more though. Get some stuff that's for the two of us," she said, warming to the idea. But she doubted that Sean was going to want to traipse through Walmart or Target buying decorations.

"Great idea. Should I send my assistant to get them?"

"He's in California, right?"

He nodded. "Yeah, but he's got contacts everywhere."

"Well, you don't have to do that. We can order it on the Target app and then just go pick it up. I want us to choose them together."

He pulled into the Christmas-tree lot and parked. "Okay. I want that too."

Sean hadn't realized how much there was still to know about Paisley. She'd done too good of a job convincing him that she was an open book, when he was beginning to realize he'd had a peek at the *Reader's Digest* condensed version. Before they'd entered the Christmas-tree farm, he'd put on a baseball cap and some Wayfarer sunglasses to help make him look not quite so recognizable. So far it was working, and he was glad.

Paisley had looked at what felt like every tree on the lot, but she kept coming back to one that was very full on one side with a few bare patches on the back. She had returned to it time and again. He knew she wanted it, that this imperfect tree appealed to her, but she didn't want to say she wanted it.

"I like this one," he said as she harrumphed a sound before turning away again.

"You do? I do too. It's so gorgeous on this side, but you know as soon as everyone walks around it, they pass it by."

He'd seen this in her from the beginning. This empathy she had for everyone. It was amazing to him that someone as soft as Paisley could be, was also a total hard-ass when it came to certain situations.

"I think that's what makes it perfect for us," he murmured, realizing as the words left his mouth that they were true.

"Why?" she asked.

"There's no ignoring the ugly parts, is there. I mean, we have good and we have bad—we all do. Somehow we've been hoodwinked into thinking we all have be perfect all the time."

She nodded. "Sorry, did you say *hoodwinked*?!"

Paisley snickered and smiled over at him, looking so cute as she teased him that he couldn't resist pulling her into his arms and kissing her. Even though he usually steered clear of PDAs, he couldn't help but cup her butt and lift her off her feet, pulling her more fully into his body. He broke the kiss after a moment before things got too heated and he wouldn't want to stop.

"So?"

She smiled up at him, the grin so wide that he felt

her joy as if it was his own. And something inside of him clenched. This wasn't a sexual-desire thing; this was a heart thing. Which he immediately slammed the door shut on and turned away to hide the happiness and fear that he felt in that instant.

"You're too cute when you say it," she said. "Should I go and get one of the attendants to get this tree packed up for us?"

"Yes. I'll stay here and keep guard so no one else nabs it."

She shook her head and chuckled as she walked away. Sean watched her go, aware that something was changing in him. He'd never felt a great shift like this before. Sometimes when he unlocked a character for a role he felt something similar, but in his real life…never.

He didn't know what it meant. Wasn't too sure he wanted to analyze it and find out. Maybe it would be better to just ignore it.

Yeah, that's what he was going to do.

The last time he thought he had emotion figured out, he'd lost Paisley and had his romantic evening ruined by the paparazzi.

It wasn't long until they had the tree strapped to the car and Paisley had the retail shopping app open on her phone. "Are you a star- or angel-on-top-of-the-tree kind of person?"

"Is there a difference? What are you?" he asked.

"I'm not sure. I think star," she said. "I like that

part of the Nativity story where the wise men are following the star."

"I like it too," he said. "Let's get a star."

She added one to the cart and then turned toward him, a strand of her hair falling forward to curl against her cheek. "Okay, this is the deal-breaker question—white lights or multicolored?"

Uh, what? Was this really a thing? "Both."

She gave him a very serious look. "You can't have both. White is all elegant and classy, multicolored is homey—"

"Multicolored," he said.

"Yay. That's what I like."

Over the next thirty minutes, he helped pick out ornaments, doing the one thing he'd never enjoyed before—shopping and spending time making decisions about something that would be on his tree.

She reached for her wallet to get her credit card to pay, but he handed her his card. "This is on me."

"You don't have to pay," she protested.

"I know. But I want to," he said. "Where now?"

"Well, we can't pick this up for a couple of hours," she said. "How about we go back to my place and start setting up the tree and have lunch?"

"I like that idea. What if we pay someone to pick up our order?" he asked.

She tipped her head to the side, studying him. "You like having things brought to you?"

He shrugged. "I'm sort of used to it. Mostly I don't like to tempt fate too much. So far we've had a nice day with just the two of us and no fans. I'd like it to stay that way. Also, the more I'm out, the better chance that paparazzi will find out about you."

"They already know about me," she reminded him.

"They know I have a woman in my life, but not your name," he said. "I don't want to put your privacy at risk."

"Okay. I can ask a runner we use at work to pick up our order. Will that work?"

"Yes. Now then, let's go see if we can get this tree up the stairwell," he told her.

"I think I could relent and use the elevator this once."

"You think so?" he asked, teasing her as he realized that for the first time in his life he wasn't thinking about how he was coming off and was just being himself.

It felt good.

Eleven

Paisley decided not to worry and just enjoy this moment with Sean. She put the Disney Channel Holiday Album on her home assistant speaker, blasting the music of her childhood as they unboxed the ornaments and started decorating the tree. Sean sang along with the tunes, proving he remembered them too.

She cocked her head to study him as he put on a Boba Fett ornament. Sean had surprised her by insisting that they order *Star Wars*-themed ornaments. And since she was getting all the Disney Princesses, she thought it was fair.

"Do you ever think about not acting?"

"For me it's not about the fame. I love the acting.

I like getting into someone else's skin and bringing them to life."

"That's probably why you've won so many awards."

He shrugged and then shook his head. "Each award gives me a bit more freedom to choose projects that resonate with me.

"Is that how you feel about brand management?" he asked her, brushing the back of his hand against her breast as he hung an ornament.

She turned, tipping back her head so she could see him. There was a slight bit of stubble on his jaw and he was looking at the tree, not her. God, he was so hot she wanted to toss aside the ornaments, lead him to the couch and make love to him. Maybe it was the pregnancy hormones making her hornier than normal or maybe it was just Sean.

"What do we do next?" he asked. "This tree is… interesting."

"It sort of feels like you and me. Not like something that someone thought would look good in a glossy magazine spread that features celebrity holiday homes."

He laughed and pulled her into his arms, kissing her. "Definitely not. I mean, I do like fresh, modern decor and my houses do suit my personality, but this is much homier."

"Like me," she said quietly.

"Yeah, just like you."

He turned her in his arms and tipped up her chin

with his finger under it. "You are a blend of so many different things that make you unique."

She flushed at the compliment. "I wouldn't change anything about you, either."

"Liar," he said, not unkindly.

"Okay, well, you're right. I wish you weren't so famous, but at the same time, I know you wouldn't be the man you are without it."

He leaned back, holding her by her waist. "Very wise."

"I know," she said, tossing her hair. "I think I could keep the magi company and hold my own. Let me grab a blanket to put under the tree."

Paisley dashed into her bedroom and into the closet where she had the box of childhood things her mom had sent her a few years ago. She'd still been mad at her family back then, so she'd shoved it back here. Sighing, she opened the lid and the scents of pine and oranges assailed her. She closed her eyes for a minute, letting the memories flow through her. She didn't want the past to interfere with the present, but she knew the past was always right there.

"Need a hand?"

She turned to see Sean standing in the doorway. "Nah."

She shifted aside homemade chains made of red and green construction paper and found the blanket. "Here it is."

"I like this too," he said, reaching around her and taking the paper chain. "Can we put this on the tree?"

She thought for a minute. All these years pretending the past was only something she had to make up for and not something that she'd enjoyed…it was as if she had been punishing herself for the family she'd had once she'd learned it wasn't perfect.

"Yes."

She went to the kitchen and started to make hot chocolate because her gut was saying this was the moment to tell Sean about the baby. The day had faded into evening and they had decided to order in pizza from Lou Malnati's, but that wasn't going to arrive for a bit. Thinking of her past made her consider her future. How she wanted it to be, and she knew she wanted that family she'd always dreamed of. She wanted it with Sean.

"Can that wait?" he asked, coming into the kitchen.

"Sure." She turned off the milk she'd started to boil and turned to face him. "What's up?"

"I need your help with something in here."

"Okay," she said.

The living room had been transformed into a magical Christmassy place. He'd lowered the overhead lights and only the tree and the lighted garland over her electric fireplace were lighting the room. He'd changed the music to a selection of jazzy instrumental holiday tunes and she noticed that he'd taken some pillows from the couch and placed them close to the tree.

"It's beautiful," she breathed.

He stopped and drew her into his arms from behind her, resting his chin on her shoulder as he put his hands around her middle. He couldn't know it, but his hands were right over their child. She felt nervous and scared, but the heat of his body behind hers soothed her.

They fit perfectly together, despite their height difference, which was something she'd rarely experienced in real life before Jack/Sean had come into her life. She knew that more than anything she was going to continue to struggle to trust him. The more he honest he was the more vulnerable she. She wished she could just let go of the past and enjoy this Christmas with him.

"This," he said, gesturing around the living room, "is making me want to kiss you."

"It is?"

He gave a small laugh. "Mmm-hmm. You've sort of been seducing me all day. With your Disney Princess ornaments and Disney Channel stars music."

"What?"

"Yup, it's like you wanted me to ravish you under the lights of our tree," he said.

"Perhaps I do." She loved this fun, lighthearted moment between them, and knew that she was falling in love with him. That there was a chance he was the man she'd always wanted to share her life with.

Before she could think about that anymore, he turned her toward him, bent down and pressed his lips to hers. His mouth on hers was firm and he took his time kissing her, rubbing his lips back and forth over hers lightly until her mouth parted and she felt the warmth of his exhalation in her mouth. He tasted so…delicious, she thought. She wanted more and invited him closer.

She thrust her tongue into his mouth and rubbed it over his teeth, and then his tongue. He bit down gently on her tongue and sucked on it. She shivered and went up on her tiptoes to get closer to him.

His taste was as addicting as hot cocoa and she wanted more him. Not just at the holidays, but always. She was just going to have to trust him and herself.

Paisley put her hands on his shoulders and then higher, rubbing her hands over his skull. His natural hair color stood out, and as much as this was familiar, there was something still new about being with Sean.

For a moment she let the thought of her secret into her mind…but he tasted so good that she didn't want to think. She just wanted to enjoy this.

He lifted the hem of her sweater up and over her head. She stood there in front of him in her festive red bra, shivering a little because there was a slight chill in the air. But then his hands warmed her as they moved over her shoulders, his fingers tracing a delicate pattern over the globes of her breasts. He moved them back and forth over the tops until the very tips of his fingers dipped beneath the cup of her bra, brushing over the edge of her nipple.

Sensual tremors coursed through her body as his fingers continued to move slowly over her. Then he caressed her arms, taking her wrists in his hands and stepping back.

She was proud of her body and wondered at the changes that pregnancy was bringing to it. His gaze started at the top of her head and moved down her neck and chest to her nipped-in waist. He planted his hands on her hips and drew her to him, lifting her. "Wrap your legs around me."

She complied. "I do like it when you hold me this way," she said as he lifted her off her feet.

He kneeled down and laid her back on the pillows under the tree. The scent of the pine fragrance sticks she'd put in the tree surrounded them as he sat back and took off his own shirt. He leaned forward, his mouth latched on her breasts, his hands on her butt, and he suckled her gently, nibbling at her nipples with his mouth as he massaged her backside. When he took her nipple into his mouth, she felt everything inside of her tighten and her center grow moist.

His mouth… She couldn't even think. She could only *feel* the shimmering sensations washing over her as he continued to feast on her breasts.

One of his heavy thighs parted her legs and nudged them apart, and then he was between them. She felt the ridge of his cock rubbing against her pleasure center and she shifted against him to increase the stimulation.

She wanted to touch him, had to hold him to her as his mouth moved from her breast down her sternum and to her belly button. He looked up at her and for a moment, when their gazes met, there was something in his eyes she couldn't read. But she felt like their relationship was changing and getting deeper.

Sean lowered his head and nibbled at the skin of her belly, his tongue tracing the indentation of her belly button and it felt like each time he dipped his tongue into her that her clit tingled. She shifted her hips to rub against him and he answered her with a thrust of his own hips.

His mouth moved lower on her, his hands drifting to the waistband of her jeans and undoing the button and then slowly lowering the zipper. She felt the warmth of his breath on her lower belly and then the edge of his tongue as he traced the skin revealed by the opening.

The feel of his five-o'clock shadow against her was soft and smooth. She moaned a little, afraid to say his name and wake from this dream, where he was hers. She knew she had so much more to learn about Sean but his raw sexuality felt familiar.

"Lift your hips," he commanded.

She planted her feet on the bed and lifted them up, then felt him draw her jeans over her hips and down her thighs. She was left wearing the tiny matching red panties she'd put on this morning.

He palmed her through the panties and she squirmed on the pillows, letting her head fall back. "I need more of you, Sean."

"How much more?"

"Everything. Give me all of you."

He gave it to her. His hand caressed her mound and then, with his mouth, he pulled down her underwear with his teeth. His hands kept moving over her stomach and thighs until she was completely naked and bare underneath him. Then he leaned back on his knees and just stared down at her.

"I was afraid you'd never let me do this again," he said.

His voice was low and husky and made her blood flow heavier in her veins. Everything about this man seemed to make her hotter and hornier than she'd ever been before.

"Me too," she said in a raspy voice. "It's never been like this with anyone else."

"Good. I want everything between us to be better."

He spoke against her skin so that she felt his words reverberate all the way through her body. He lowered his head again and rubbed his chin over her mound. Just a back-and-forth motion that made her clit feel engorged.

He parted her with the thumb and forefinger of his left hand and she felt the air against her most intimate flesh, and then the brush of his tongue. It

was so soft and wet, and she squirmed, wanting—
no, *needing*—more from him.

As if reading her mind, he scraped his teeth over
her and she almost came right then. But he lifted his
head and smiled up her body at her. By this time she
knew her lover well enough to know that he liked to
draw out the experience.

She gripped his shoulders as he teased her with
his mouth and then she tunneled her fingers through
his hair, holding him closer to her as she lifted her
hips. He moaned against her and the sound sent chills
racing through her body.

His other hand traced her opening. Those large
deft fingers making her squirm against him. Her
breasts felt full and her nipples were tight as he
pushed just the tip of his finger inside of her.

The first ripples of her orgasm started to pulse
through her, but he pulled back, lifting his head and
moving down her body, then nibbling at the flesh of
her legs. She was aching for him. Needed more of
what he had been giving her.

"Sean…"

"Yes?" he asked, lightly stroking her lower belly
and then moving both hands to her breasts, where
he cupped the full globes.

"I need more of you."

"Don't worry, Pais. You're going to get all of me,"
he said.

She was shivering with the need to come and
wanted more from him. She just wanted his big body

moving over hers. Ached to have his cock inside of her. She reached between their bodies and stroked him through his pants. Then slowly lowered the tab of the zipper, but he caught her wrist and drew her hand up above her head.

"Feels. So. Good," she purred as he lowered his body over hers so his bare chest rubbed against hers. Then his thigh was between her legs, moving slowly against her engorged flesh, and she wanted to scream as everything in her tightened just a little bit more. But he didn't stay there, just kissed her lips, intimately, and then moved down her body again.

He drove himself into her in one long thrust and she writhed against him but he just slowed his strokes and pivoted his hips so that the sensations were even more intense than before. She opened her eyes to look up at him and this time she knew she saw something different.

The first wave of orgasm rolled through her body.

Her hips jerked forward and her nipples tightened. She felt the moisture between her legs and his one thrust growing deeper and faster. She was shivering and her entire body was convulsing but he didn't stop. He kept driving into her harder and harder until they came together in a screaming orgasm.

Stars blended with the lights of the Christmas tree, and she wanted to claw at his shoulders as pleasure rolled over her. It was more than she could process and she had to close her eyes. She reached for

Sean, needing some sort of comfort after that storm of ecstasy.

He pulled her into his arms and rocked her back and forth. "New tradition. I can't wait to see what else you inspire me to do this Christmas."

She opened her eyes, looking up into his, and she realized that if she didn't tell him about the baby at this moment, she was going to lose him forever. The words were there but sort of stuck in the back of her throat. Then the doorbell rang and Sean leaned down to kiss her before getting to his feet and refastening his jeans.

"I'll get that."

She watched him leave with a heavy heart. He'd opened himself up to her and shown her that she could trust him but still she hesitated. She knew she couldn't wait much longer, not only for hers and the baby's sake, but for Sean's too.

Twelve

"Ugly-sweater party!" Delaney exclaimed as she opened the front door of the home that she shared with Nolan and his six-year-old daughter, Daisey. Delaney and Daisey were wearing matching sweaters that were possibly the ugliest holiday sweaters that Paisley had ever seen, she thought as she entered. Red, green and gold knit had been embellished with hand-sewn gold bells and stars all over it.

Delaney lived in a large mansion with her fiancé, Nolan, who was an aerospace entrepreneur.

"Woo-hoo," Paisley said. "You two look super cute."

She handed her bestie the bottle of champagne she had brought as a hostess gift and then bent down to

Daisey's eye level and offered her the present she'd brought for her.

"Thank you, Paisley. Do I have to wait until Christmas to open it?" Daisey asked.

Paisley glanced up at Delaney, who nodded.

"Yes."

"Darn it!" Daisey grumbled.

"Why don't you go put it under the tree and let your daddy know that Paisley is here?"

As soon as Daisey was out of the hallway, Delaney turned to her. "Where's Sean? Did he decide to ditch and head back to the West Coast?"

The door opened behind her as Delaney finished her sentence.

"No, I didn't. I'm assuming you meant me."

"I did, indeed," Delaney said. "But it was sort of tongue-in-cheek. I'm nervous tonight. I sent my dad an invitation sort of as a joke and he RSVP'd."

Paisley started laughing at her friend. Delaney's father was a very buttoned-down aristocratic sort of man who had never really approved of Delaney and her wild ways, but since she'd settled down with Nolan the two had gotten closer.

"It'll be funny to see him in an ugly Christmas sweater," Sean said.

"Yeah, about that. Why are you two wearing matching *Christmas Magic* movie sweaters?" Delaney asked.

"They are a bit over-the-top. I mean, who wears

a sweater promoting themselves?" Sean asked with a smile.

The door opened and Dante and Olive walked in, both wearing matching Inferno Brewing sweaters, which made Delaney howl with laughter. "All of my friends apparently. Come in and let's get this party started with some cocktails—"

"Hey, I sent cases of Inferno over," Dante said.

"And beer. Sheesh." She led them into the living room, which was party-ready with a huge, beautifully decorated tree in one corner with presents underneath it. There was a bar set up in the opposite corner and a deejay just to the left. The furniture had been rearranged and small conversation areas had been assembled.

Delaney waved them off as the caterer came to ask her a question. Sean slipped his hand into Paisley's as Dante and Olive offered to get them drinks and headed off to the bar. "I didn't realize this was going to be a big party."

"Would you have ditched me if you had?" she asked.

"No, but I might have dyed my hair and come as Jack," he quipped.

"Jack's been banished to the past," she said tartly.

"Don't worry—he's not coming back," Sean assured her. "Do you know how many people will be here?"

"If it's anything like her last party, not too many, and she usually just invites good friends and some of her relatives. Some of them are more famous than you," Paisley said.

"Great. I don't care about that. I just wanted to have some fun with my girl."

"Your girl?"

"Aren't you?" he murmured.

She turned to face him, leaning up on her tiptoes. "I thought I'd proven I'm a woman."

"Touché. But you know what I meant. Are you mine?" he asked.

His. Was she? She wanted to be. But she knew as long as her secret was between them, she couldn't. Not really. "I'd like to be."

"Good. That's all I needed to know," he said, kissing her.

His tongue tangled with hers and she wished they were alone in her bedroom. Maybe then she'd find the courage that being in his arms always gave her to finally tell him about the baby.

"Enough of that. Take these drinks before Delaney tries to rope us into greeting guests," Olive said as they returned.

They took their drinks and toasted each other. "To the cutest twinning couples in the room."

"Hear! Hear!"

Sean and Dante kept the conversation going and Paisley couldn't help but notice how well he fit in with her friends. Any fears she had of him being too cool for her inner circle were gone. She was running out of reasons not to tell him he was going to be a daddy. Her last hang-up—that he was still not being real with her—was just not justified and she knew it.

The hang-up was really her own fear. She hated that she'd trusted him when he was Jack. Hated that her own father had made promises each time he'd been busted to come clean and then started grifting again as soon as they got to a new town. She had a history of forgiving too many times and she knew the situation with Sean was different. Well, in her head she might now that, but her heart wasn't so sure.

"Karaoke?" Dante asked.

"What? Sorry I was thinking about the press event tomorrow night," Paisley lied.

Sean gave her a look as if to ask if she was okay and she nodded slightly.

"I was just saying that Delaney has some games planned and one of them is paired-up karaoke," Olive explained.

"Oh, bring it on! We should do good because Sean's got a great voice," Paisley bragged.

"Yeah, you should," Olive agreed.

"Hey, I'm not that bad," Dante said.

"You're actually the best," Olive crooned, turning toward him. "I love your voice. Sean's going to have to work hard to beat you."

"When did this become a competition between us?" Sean mused. "Dante, I think we should pair up against the ladies…"

"If you think you can beat us. Paisley and I can bring it," Olive warned the men.

"Only after several shots of tequila," Paisley joked.

"Challenge accepted," Dante said.

Paisley laughed and knew that this night was going to be a lot of fun. But a part of her wished there could be a clear sign that Sean was really going to stay. That he'd be the partner she wanted and needed him to be to help raise her baby.

The next two weeks flew by and Sean found himself starting to believe that his relationship with Paisley might last beyond the holidays. They'd spent their time with her friends, and his assistant and his girlfriend flew out for a weekend as a surprise and were planning to return on the 23rd. They'd done the press events that Paisley had outlined for them. Tonight was the premiere of the Christmas movie and he was looking forward to it. In the film, he played a prince in disguise who falls in love with a girl he meets at the airport.

Not so different from his real-life chance meeting with Paisley in the coffee shop.

Sean dressed carefully in his custom tuxedo for the event, because unlike the big romantic date he'd arranged for Paisley the night the paparazzi had ambushed him, this was going to be the real thing. He knew now that he'd been playacting when it came to himself and Paisley. Though he believed he'd genuinely cared for her, his emotions hadn't been fully realized and it was only over these last few weeks, when they'd truly gotten to know each other, that he'd come to understand that.

He made a few plans for the evening but knew that those plans could change depending on Paisley. He'd asked her to let him gift her a dress for the evening and she'd agreed. He'd called his designer friend and sent some photos of Paisley, and Dimitri had sent the outfit directly to her along with shoes and wrap.

Sean couldn't wait to see the dress on her when he went to pick her up. They'd spent equal amounts of time at his rented house on Lake Michigan and at her apartment. She'd insisted on decorating a tree at his house and this time they'd gone with a color scheme. All red, green and gold ornaments. He glanced over at it as he checked his tie one last time before he left.

This rented house had a dozen touches that were all Paisley. The key tray by the front door. A framed photo of the two of them in their matching sweaters at Olive's party, along with a picture of himself, Nolan and Dante holding a tacky gold microphone that Olive had made into a trophy when they'd won the karaoke contest.

For the first time in memory, this place felt like home, and it was because of Paisley.

Tonight he wanted to take some time with her. Do a gut check and make sure he was really falling for her and then...well, ask her to make this permanent. He didn't know what that looked like. He hadn't been raised in a traditional family, but he had slowly let himself start thinking of having one. It had been a long time coming, but now he could finally admit to himself he did want a wife and maybe kids someday with Paisley. She was everything he needed and yet something he hadn't known he wanted.

Until now.

The doorbell pinged and he pulled on his topcoat before stepping out to find the car and driver the studio had sent awaiting him.

"Evening, sir. I hope I'm not too early."

"You're right on time. We might have to wait when we get to Ms. Campbell's place," Sean said, knowing that in spite of her good intentions, Paisley was always running behind.

"You're the star. I think they'll wait for you," the driver assured him.

Sean sat in the back of the car with the privacy window up just because he was too much in his own head. He wanted this date to be perfect, and thought of the ring he had in his pocket and what it meant to him.

Had he misread her? For the first time, the gift he'd always taken for granted—his ability to read another person—felt hazy. He wondered if it was his own feelings interfering.

Whatever it was, he'd never been this nervous before a date…or a premiere. He knew he wasn't worried about the film. Early screening audiences and reviews had been positive. So these jitters must be stemming from his feelings toward Paisley.

She'd changed him. Helped him finally figure out

how to be himself in the real world. With people who weren't industry insiders or on a film set. He was being just Sean and felt truly accepted for the first time in his life.

That was a gift that he didn't truly appreciate. It was something that he knew he wasn't totally comfortable with but he was getting much closer to that.

The car pulled up in front of Paisley's building and there were a few photographers out front. But for once, he didn't brush past them. He smiled and waved, then called for them to get tickets to see his movie before he went inside and up the stairs to her apartment.

He knocked on the door, seeing the wreath that they'd made together with Daisey—Nolan's six-year-old daughter. She'd learned how to make it in school by weaving together cutouts of their hands out of red and green construction paper. Paisley had then used her Instax printer to put pictures of all of them on the wreath. This was the family he'd never had and had secretly always wanted, he thought as he looked at those faces.

And he'd only found them through Paisley.

He knocked on the door and heard her call out that she was coming. Then the door opened and his breath caught in his chest as he looked at her in the slim-fitting velvet dress trimmed with pearls at the neck. Her hair was up, with tendrils that framed her heart-shaped face, and she smiled at him.

And the world stopped.

He loved her.

That was why he was so nervous about this night. Why it needed to be perfect. He loved her and he knew it was at once the most fabulous and the scariest thing he'd ever felt.

"You're gorgeous."

She winked at him. "You too. I mean, I knew you cleaned up well, but—"

He leaned in and kissed her, not because he didn't want the compliment, but because he felt the urge to blurt out that he loved her and he wasn't sure he was ready for her to know.

Sean kissing her in the doorway had set the tone of the night. He'd swept her down the stairs to the car and waiting driver, yet when they arrived at the premiere, she pushed aside all swoony thoughts about her smoking-hot date and gone to work. She had a list of the reporters who would be on the red carpet.

"Ready for this?"

The red carpet had been set up under arches, which made for a winter-wonderland vibe. They had trees spaced down the length to give each interview some privacy.

"Yeah, I actually don't mind this bit," he said with a wink. "But are *you* ready?"

"I've got the easy part. Pointing you at the reporters," she replied.

The door opened and the driver offered her his hand as she stepped out onto the red carpet. The crowds were waiting and as soon as Sean climbed out behind her, there was a burst of flashbulbs and calls of his name, and some applause. He waved to them all and put his hand on the small of her back, but instead of just walking past the fans who'd lined up—probably for hours—to see him, he stopped and shook their hands and posed for photos.

Paisley acted as photographer for a few of them. She was impressed by his willingness to talk to all of the fans that were there. He didn't rush them or brush them off—it was, to her, a mark of the man. It reinforced what she had been starting to believe about him.

For as much as Sean was a big Hollywood star, he was a genuine man. He might be used to luxury houses, hired drivers and just asking for something and expecting it to get delivered to him, but there was also something about him that was very down-to-earth.

"The first reporter is from our local Chicago news outlet," she told him. "I think she might be the source behind Wend-Z, so she's going to probably ask you some of the more salacious questions. I'll stay close and signal me if you need me to interrupt."

Wend-Z was a local gossip site that had was the bane of Delaney's existence and hadn't made Sean's life too easy since his cover had been blown. She just seemed to always have a tantalizing bit of gossip.

"I can handle her. I've been asked more inappropriate questions than you'd believe," he said. He squeezed her hand and then put on what she thought of as his I'm-a-megastar smile and walked over to the reporter.

Paisley kept her distance, trying to keep her focus on the evening, but it was impossible not to think of the baby and the fact that she hadn't told Sean about it yet. Seeing him in his element, working the crowd, made her very aware that as different as their lives were, this wasn't a situation that she wasn't going to be able to handle.

And as they moved down the red carpet, she could easily envision the two of them working together at future premieres. The last few weeks had been magical. The kind of Christmas that she hadn't known was possible. They'd done press events and stuff with her found family and even Mrs. B had invited them over to watch her favorite film, *Miracle on 34th Street.*

After that, it had been impossible for Paisley not to acknowledge that she had no real fears about Sean faking it with her. He was more real than her father had ever been. But still she kept quiet about the pregnancy.

Being sure of Sean as a man was one thing. But being sure of him as a father, that was something else entirely.

They'd never even talked about staying together after the holidays. What if he went back to LA after the New Year? But she didn't think he'd just disappear.

He'd gotten a script just two days ago and told her he'd be filming in Vancouver from February until May. Almost as an aside, he'd suggested she come visit him, but his eyes had been serious. Which indicated he was as unsure about the two of them as she was.

She'd told him she'd come visit, hoping he'd say he wanted them to be a couple. But he hadn't. So she wasn't sure where he saw their relationship going.

It was ridiculous to let fear take so much control over her life with him, but there it was. She was afraid to say she cared for him, afraid to admit how much she wanted him in her life because she was terrified of his reaction when she told him she was pregnant.

Now she wished she'd blurted it out on the same night that he'd found out his real identity. But, of course, she hadn't, and she couldn't go back in time or even call for a do-over.

However, knowing how betrayed she'd felt when she'd found out he'd lied…how could she justify not saying anything to him about the baby?

"That's it. I'm yours for the evening, Paisley. Let's get a picture together and then head into the premiere."

She smiled at him but some of her joy in the evening was dimmed because of her own actions. She had to tell him.

Maybe she should whisper it in his ear when he pulled her close for a photo in front of the movie-poster backdrop the studio had provided. "I have something I want to talk to you about."

He looked down at her and smiled that intimate just-for-her smile. "Me too. After the party?"

She nodded, secretly grateful for another reprieve, but at the same time she knew that the more time she took to tell him, the harder it was going to be for him to hear. But then his director came over and Paisley stepped aside to let them get a photo together. She stood on the sidelines watching and hoping that she hadn't waited too long to tell Sean, because she knew that losing him for real would hurt more deeply than her father's betrayal, than losing her childhood home. Losing Sean would mean forfeiting the only man she'd ever really let herself trust.

Thirteen

Sean's Christmas movie premiere had been a lot of fun and the after party was at an exclusive Chicago club ballroom. They'd all been shuttled over after watching the movie and now were walking around what looked like the interior ballroom of the prince's castle from Sean's movie. Sean was talking to some studio executives and Paisley stepped outside to get a break from the noise and crowds. She stayed close by, though, because she didn't know anyone in this world.

As happy as she was that he had fit into her world, she wasn't so sure that she fit into his. This kind of party wasn't like anything she was used to. She'd worked a few events like this with her clients, but generally once the press left, she did too.

"Hey, lady, what are you doing out here?"

"Just taking a breather. Your movie is great. You were the best part," she said.

"I was?" He arched one eyebrow at her as he pulled her into his arms. She heard the sounds of Elton John's "Step into Christmas" coming from inside the ballroom. "Are you a tiny bit biased?"

"Definitely. I mean you're the only movie star I know," she murmured.

"Is that why you like me?"

"No!" she insisted, putting her hands on his face. It was so much more complicated than that. "I'm not chasing fame."

"I know. I was just teasing. Want to dance?" he asked. "I can't stay out here or the party will move out here."

She wrapped her arms around him and looked up into his eyes, realizing she was always going to have to share him with the world. But she'd known that all along. Right?. She went up on tiptoe and kissed him. He sighed and pulled her closer, his hands on her waist as his tongue brushed over hers. She wanted this moment to never end.

But it had to because this was his premiere party and she had to tell him about the baby before this moment could be truly real.

"Sure," she said, thinking he might be exaggerating about people following him outside, but as they started back into the ballroom, three or four groups of people were coming out in the hall.

"There you are! After this song is over we need you to get up there and give your speech." The elegantly dressed woman turned to Paisley. "Hello, there, I'm Cass Genaro. We spoke on Zoom. So nice to meet you," she said, holding her hand out to Paisley.

"Nice to meet you in person." Cass said. She was one of the studio execs who had set up all of Sean's press with Paisley.

"I'll show you to your table while Sean is doing his thing. He's got about two more things to take care of at this party and then he's yours," Cass said. "Until then, I'll hang with you."

Sean glanced down at her as if asking if she was okay. She smiled weakly and nodded. "Sounds like fun. Lead on, Cass."

Sean stopped her with his hand on her shoulder and leaned in to kiss her. "Thanks for understanding."

"It's no big deal. I like seeing you do your thing."

She followed Cass to a table toward the front of the room, where several of the executives that she'd seen Sean with earlier were already seated. There was also the husband of Sean's costar. He was making small talk with the execs and Paisley got a glimpse of what her life might be if she and Sean made this work.

Apparently she was going to have to do this kind

of thing at all the movie parties. She smiled at the others and decided that this was a good test to see if she was up to it. But deep down, she was nervous and didn't really know what to do. Then she remembered Sean jumping in at Mrs. B's and decorating cookies, and singing karaoke with Dante and Nolan. This was her trial by fire. Her chance to prove to herself that she wanted to be more than his Christmas fling.

"Hi, I'm Lorenzo," the costar's husband said in a lovely Spanish accent.

"Paisley—I'm with Sean."

"I noticed," he said with a smile. He introduced her around the table and she found that conversation went easily, and then the song ended and Sean and his costar—Desi—stepped up on a raised dais.

"Thank you, everyone, for your hard work on *Christmas Magic*. Seeing the completed film is always eye-opening. I knew we were good when we were shooting but tonight confirmed it," Sean said.

"This party is our way of saying an extra thank-you to everyone who's helped out along the way," Desi said. "We hope you enjoy it."

They continued to call out individual names and invite those people up on the stage to collect gifts and say a few words. After about thirty minutes, Sean and Desi rejoined them at the table as Cass introduced the outtakes video, which was fun and entertaining.

Sean put his arm on the back of her chair and kissed her cheek. She felt almost like he was nervous too. Unsure of something. Her? Them? She had no idea, but when she saw the behind-the-scenes Sean, she got another glimpse of the man she cared so much for. He was funny on set. Much like he was with her but different. There was a professionalism to everything he did, but he was aware he was the big name on the film and it seemed to her that he set a relaxed tone.

When the video ended they were served a light dinner and then a band came on and everyone was invited to the dance floor.

Paisley danced in Sean's arms, enjoying being there. He sang under his breath to her, then grabbed drinks from a passing waiter before and led her off the dance floor to a quiet corner under a lighted archway.

"When I invited you to dinner a few weeks ago, I wanted to be my most perfect, romantic self, and everything went to crap. I thought I needed a writer to tell me how to act, but tonight things haven't been perfect and I had to work. But honestly, Pais, I feel like this moment is almost the best I can make it.

"Having you here by my side has brought my entire life into focus and there's nothing I want more than to keep you by my side. I know…we said just for Christmas but I want more."

Joy washed over her and she didn't think of the consequences of the secret she was holding deep inside as she threw herself into his arms and kissed him.

"I'm guessing you like that idea," he said dryly.

"I do," she returned.

He handed her a champagne glass.

"A toast to us and our future," he said.

She started to lift her glass but stopped. She couldn't toast to that. Not yet. Not until she told him about the baby.

"Uh, there's something I need to tell you first…"

But before she could get the words out, they were interrupted yet again.

"O'Neill, we need you for a cast photo," Cass said.

Getting called away wasn't at all what Sean wanted. But he couldn't blow this off.

"Don't go anywhere," he said, handing her his champagne glass.

"I'll be here."

He was glad for the excuse to get away from Paisley before he said something that was either more than he wanted to say, or somehow wrong in the moment. His emotions were running high and for the first time with her he felt vulnerable. Because if she didn't feel the same way, if she was just hanging out with him to get through the holiday season…

He'd get it, but damn, it would hurt.

No one wanted to be alone at Christmas. There had never been a truer thought in his mind than that. But he wanted to believe after the magical night they'd spent together that there was something more between them. But she'd said she wanted to be with him. So what could she have to say?

He was pulled in front of a Christmas tree with the rest of the cast by Cass. Desi was positioned next to him.

"I like Paisley. Lorenzo said she slayed the execs too. Looks like you found a keeper," Desi whispered.

"Yeah, she's great," Sean said. But now, he wasn't sure. What did she want to talk to him about? He smiled for the photo but the sense of this being a perfect night was fading. He'd never been one to search for this kind of happiness, had always thought it was out of reach. Had he fooled himself? Had he allowed himself to be swayed by her sweet face? And her broken past?

He had connected to her as much in the present as he had with the shared pain of their childhoods. Different stories and different paths, but it had led them both, he thought, to each other.

"Let's do one with the crew," Cass called.

Sean kept smiling, but in his heart he felt panic. Why had he allowed himself to strip himself emotionally bare like this? Then he stopped himself. Was this what Paisley had felt when she'd heard his real name? When she'd learned he wasn't Jack? At this moment, he had no idea what she was going to tell him—only that she had something she wanted to talk about.

Was he borrowing trouble?

Didn't he always?

His gut instinct was to look at it from every angle.

The past had taught him to keep his back up, and with Paisley he'd let it down.

He'd fallen for her and made her into the hometown sweetheart that he'd never encountered before. Couldn't he trust that's what she was? At least until she proved otherwise?

"That's all, folks. You're free for the evening. Don't forget to collect your swag bags on the way home and have a merry Christmas," Cass said.

Desi hugged him and then went to join Lorenzo, and he saw Paisley standing there under the lighted arch watching him and waiting. He walked back over to her.

"So you wanted to tell me something?"

She bit down on her lip. "Well, I…"

"You okay?" he asked.

"Yeah… I just think I didn't realize what your life is really like. I mean, is this…? Never mind. I don't want to ruin our evening."

He knew that like him, she was feeling her way through this relationship. Things had been so much easier for him as Jack. Because Jack had no commitments, no fans and no real life. "Let's go find a quiet place for this talk."

She raised both eyebrows at him. "I said never mind."

"Yeah, but we both know that you don't mean never mind. Let's get out of here and head back home."

"Yours or mine?"

"Either," he said, but didn't say out loud that both felt like theirs. He wasn't as sure now as he'd been before.

He led her out of the ballroom as their driver texted he was out front. They got into the back of the car.

As they started to pull away, she tipped her head to the side. "There is something a little odd about how well you know me."

"We lived with each other for months."

"I know, but now that you're you, it's…well, different."

"Fair enough," he said. "I'm glad for that time we had before. It was easier."

She tipped her head to the side, pursing her lips. "Because it wasn't real."

"What is real?" he prodded, mainly to see if he could distract her.

"Do you really want to talk about philosophy and perceptions of reality?" she asked.

"No, but sort of. I mean it does seem easier to discuss abstract theories than to talk about us."

She gave a little laugh. "So true. But here's the thing…" She clenched her hands together in her lap. "Okay, I'm just going to say it without trying to figure out if I should or not. All right?"

That sounded…not good. "Sure."

"You are never really going to be able to live here with me, are you? I mean you can stay here for Christmas but this isn't your life."

He leaned against the seat and looked out the window and the passing Chicago skyline as the driver turned down the familiar road that led to her apartment. No, he couldn't live here in her apartment in Chicago. He needed more privacy than her place afforded, but a part of him wanted to live with Paisley and he didn't really see a scenario where she moved to LA.

"Your apartment, well, no, but here in Chicago with you, I think yes. That's what I was suggesting."

"I need you to be totally honest with me. Are you serious right now?"

"I am. But I have a feeling that you've been reassured in the past by your dad so that might not really help…" Sean knew that for the both of them, relationships were hard. He was secretive by nature and for practicality's sake. Whereas she needed the blunt brutal truth all the time after being raised by a man who lied to her and everyone else.

"Is this going to be a deal breaker for us?" he asked at last.

She chewed her lower lip and he remembered how her mouth felt under his and how much he wanted her back in his arms. He was trying his best to be the man she needed. One who didn't say the wrong thing and was honest. But the truth was, he felt more at home behind the facade of a role. And that wasn't an option now.

"I want it too," she said. "Tonight was…one of

the best nights of my life. I don't want to screw it up now by being too me, but I'm a worrier."

"You aren't screwing anything up. I like that you worry. I know you do it because you care."

She reached out, putting her hand over his. "I do care about you, Sean. Please, never doubt that."

That statement made the hair on the back of his neck stand up. Why would he doubt her?

Luckily, the car pulled up in front of her building. They went up to her apartment before she had to say anything else. She was aware of him quietly walking behind her, and also aware that she hadn't said the simple words, *I'm pregnant*. That's all she had to do.

It was literally that easy.

But instead she was talking about everything else, frantically trying to find the right way to tell him the truth. Like she feared that once he knew, it would irrevocably change things between them. But as they got into her apartment and she saw the tree they'd decorated together, she remembered how he'd made love to her beneath all those glittering lights, and honestly, she felt so in love with him at this very moment.

In love.

That was it. She loved him. No more pretending that maybe she didn't because he'd deceived her about who he really was. No more believing that she couldn't trust him because of that lie. No more trying to convince herself that she didn't want to spend the rest of her life with this man at her side.

"Doubt you? That's an odd thing to say."

She swallowed. Why had she put it that way? It was like she wanted him to push her so she'd have no excuse but to tell him the truth because she was too cowardly to do it on her own.

"I know. It's just...remember when I said that there was something I needed to tell you but wasn't ready?"

He lifted both eyebrows at her as he took off his coat. "I do. Are you ready now?"

Paisley looked down at her lap. She knew that the options were limited. *Yes or no.* Either way, this moment was a big one. "I'm not sure."

"What's stopping you?"

"You."

"Me?" he asked incredulously. "Should I be worried?"

Yes, very worried. She had no idea how he was going to react to the news that she was pregnant. "I hope not."

He got up and came to stand next to her. Then he drew her to her feet and pulled her into his arms. "I know you're not sure you can trust me with the big things, Pais, but you can."

He hugged her so tightly that she almost just blurted it out, but she knew this was a betrayal and he was going to feel it as such. The same way that he must have felt trapped at times by being Jack around her. And sure, it would be easy to try to justify her silence by using his actions as an excuse. But she couldn't. Sean deserved to know.

She tipped back her head and saw he was watching her, waiting. He rubbed his thumbs over her temples and then leaned down to give her the sweetest and kindest kiss she'd ever received. With that one embrace, it was as if he was saying *trust me, I'm here for you.*

She felt tears sting her eyes. She knew he was here. He was being way too nice to her. She needed to just tell him what was going on and then... Then she'd be able to move on. The not knowing how he was going to react was making her—

Crap.

She felt bile rising in the back of her throat and knew she was going to throw up.

"Be right back."

She ran from the kitchen to the hallway bathroom, making it just in time. Until the pregnancy she hadn't thrown up since her college days, when she'd partied a bit too hard. When she was finished, she rinsed her mouth out and then brushed her teeth, carefully avoiding looking at the doorway, where Sean was leaning against the jamb trying to look casual, but the worry in his eyes belied his pose.

"Are you okay?"

"Yes. I think I drank too much."

"Now who is lying?" he stated. "You didn't drink anything but seltzer water."

She rubbed the back of her hand over her mouth. She couldn't wait another minute. She needed him to know and she'd run out of excuses.

"I am okay," she said at last. "I've, um, been trying to figure out how to tell you this and there is no way to ease into it."

"Are you really sick?" he asked worriedly. "I mean, cancer or something? I have a lot of resources... We will get you the best help there is."

He took her hand in his and led her out of the bathroom to the couch in the living room. The Christmas tree and the multicolored lights twinkled, giving the room a warm and cozy feel.

He pulled her down on the couch next to him then into the curve of his side so he could hold her. "No wonder you didn't want to say anything. It's okay. I'm not going anywhere. I'll be here by your side."

Oh. God. He was making it worse. For a brief second, she wondered if she could just pretend that she was seriously ill but rejected that immediately. That lie was too big, too cruel, and Sean deserved better.

"Thank you."

She shifted on the couch and turned so she was facing him. "I'm not ill. I'm...pregnant."

His brow furrowed and he sort of stared at her like she had spoken a foreign language. Then she saw him get it and his face turned hard and he got to his feet, pacing away from the couch. He turned and looked at her.

"How long have you known?" he said shortly.

"Since the night I found out you weren't Jack."

He nodded. "Fair play. I mean I lied to you so you sort of owed me."

"I didn't owe you," she said hoarsely. "I didn't know you. There's a difference."

"I'm trying to see it, Paisley."

She knew that he was. He just stood there on the other side of the living room in his tuxedo, watching her, and the lights of their tree didn't seem so comforting now.

Fourteen

Pregnant?

Fuck.

A father.

He had no actual idea how to be a father. His own had left when Sean was a toddler and he had no memory of the man. He hadn't even tried to come back into Sean's life when he got famous. And his mother…well, she hadn't exactly been parent of the year. In fact, she never wanted to be a parent. She'd admitted as much. She would have left too, but someone had to stay for him.

He'd been a burden to her.

He looked at Paisley. There was so much to unpack but he thought of his child. *His child.* His mind was still racing. He wouldn't let that child feel abandoned, or like a burden.

"This difference…does it somehow involve our baby?" he asked, unable to keep the sarcasm out of his voice. He was trying to see her side, and to be fair, if he wasn't angry he might be able to. But right now he saw the lie she'd told him and it was different than what he'd done.

"Yes," she said, getting up and coming over to him. "It has everything to do with the baby. I didn't know Sean O'Neill. I had no clue how much of the man I knew as Jack was actually part of you."

Damn. He knew she was making sense but he was hurt. "I told you I hadn't been lying to you."

"My dad has told me the same thing."

"I'm not your goddamn dad! I haven't deceived anyone or taken their savings and caused them to lose their homes. I'm an actor and you've seen what my life is like in public. I chose to get to know a woman I was attracted to as a man and not a celebrity. Try to see how that is different."

He stepped away from her, realizing that his anger was making him loom over her, and he never wanted to intimidate her that way. Forcing himself to take several deep breaths, he turned and walked toward the door. He should leave until he had this savage part of himself under control.

"I get it. You're right," she said. She hadn't followed him.

He turned and saw her standing there next to the

tree that, in his mind had been a real turning point for them. The moment when he'd decided that they could work. And it broke his heart. She hadn't been as honest with him as he'd been with her.

He didn't say anything because his hurt and anger made him want to keep lashing out and he wasn't sure he could contain it.

"I just didn't know you and then I started to get to know you and my gut was saying to trust you, but still… I was afraid," she choked out. "That's not fair to you but that's the reality. I wish I could say that I had some good reason but things were going well and I wanted to…well, enjoy this Christmas with you."

He put his hands on his hips and looked at the floor. "I wanted that too. But I'm falling for you, Paisley. And you were keeping this from me. I don't know how to make that right in my mind."

"I get it. I felt the same way," she admitted. "I can give you time if you think that's what you need."

"What I need…" he muttered under his breath. What was that exactly? He had no idea what he needed. "Tell me about the baby. Did you think I'd be a crap father is that part of why you hesitated?"

He looked across the room at her. She wrapped her arms around her waist and he remembered her throwing up just a minute before. "Wait, isn't morning sickness supposed to just be in the morning?"

"Yeah, I mean I haven't thrown up at night before. I think it was the stress…knowing I had to tell you, afraid of what would happen and all that."

He cursed succinctly under his breath. "Sit down. Can I get you anything?"

She shook her head as she moved to the couch and sat down again. He came over as well, sitting in an easy chair that was kitty-corner to the sofa.

"I didn't know what kind of father you'd be or if you even want to be one. Do you?"

Did he? He knew in an instant that he did. He couldn't walk away from a baby of his. Did he have a clue what to do? Hell, no, but he wasn't going to let that stop him. "Of course."

"I thought so, but at first you were someone I didn't know," she said. "I know it's a sorry excuse but on top of everything else, I had to wait."

"I get the waiting. Honestly, I do. But after carolling and the tree and the party at Delaney's…it seemed like you did get to know me and you still weren't sure."

That he realized was the crux of this situation for him. She didn't trust him. She didn't trust any man really. And until she did, they had no future. It wasn't about if he could fly back and forth to the West Coast, or if he had to be *on* when they were in public. This was a much deeper issue and she was the only one who could fix it.

"I know," she said sadly. "It's not fair to you."

"You're right, its not. So tell me about the pregnancy," he said. That was something he could focus on.

"I'm five weeks along. I have another doctor's

appointment the second week of January. I've had some morning sickness but not too bad."

"Any ideas how it happened?" he asked. He almost always used a condom.

"I think it was that party the weekend before Halloween when we got back from Olive's and—"

"We did it in the hallway and I didn't get a condom," he said.

"Yeah."

God, he'd been so hot for her, he couldn't wait to have her. Looking back, he knew it was the pressure of keeping his true identity from her while falling for her. But he hadn't realized it at the time. He'd just rearranged their clothing and taken her up against the wall.

It had been hard and fast, just pure, primal need. He hadn't been thinking…

"I need time to process this and figure out how to move forward. I want to be involved in the baby's life."

"But not mine?" she asked.

The words were ripped from the raw part of her that sort of got what he was saying, but ached at what it meant. The inner battle she'd been waging within herself had disappeared when she'd seen how hurt he was by her silence about the baby.

In that moment she'd known that he was a man she could trust with her heart and soul. But that she'd hurt him so badly he might never want that. It hadn't been easy to keep the baby from him in the last few weeks, but she'd felt she had no choice.

She had been letting the past rule her present and had totally compromised the future. With a sinking heart, she sat on her couch, looking over at Sean next to that tree they'd decorated. That was when she should have told him the truth. That moment. But…she hadn't been able to.

She could beat herself up all she wanted to about the timing but this was the first moment she'd felt like she could tell him.

And it was too late.

"I don't know," he said at last. "I need time to think. The pregnancy is somehow easier to deal with than you keeping it from me."

She nodded. "That's how I felt about working with you. I mean, it's something to focus on. So how involved do you want to be?" she asked. She was going to try to keep from crying at the loss of Sean. And there was no way back from this. She felt it in the coldness that emanated from him now and in the white-hot anger that she had seen in him before it. He wasn't acting or pretending to be anything other than a man who'd been badly hurt by her.

"All of it. I want to go to doctor's appointments— if that's okay with you—and be involved in every aspect of your pregnancy."

"Okay. I don't know what the appointments will look like, but as long as we both feel comfortable you can come." She was starting to feel numb and that wasn't good. The last time she felt this way she'd almost come undone. And this was worse. She couldn't disappear and she couldn't deny that she was to blame for this.

"I will have to get my lawyers involved in this. I want to set up funds for you and the child. Also, you can't keep living here. Once word of this gets out—"

"Why would it get out?"

He shot her a disbelieving look. "Come on, Paisley, you're not that naive. You've walked past the paparazzi outside, just as I have. Once you start showing it will be harder to protect you. I'll have Bert get in touch after the New Year and we'll get the ball rolling. For now, just text me about the appointments and all of that."

He pushed to his feet, and she noticed he kept bunching his hands into fists and unclenching them as he walked back toward the hallway that led to the front door. He was leaving and this time…it felt real. He wasn't going to be back in her life. This hurt and betrayal had gone too deep for him. And before she'd gotten to know him and had learned what his past was, she might have held out hope that he'd come back.

But she knew there wasn't a chance in hell of that.

She knew it with such deep certainty because she wouldn't be able to forgive him if the situation had been reversed. This wasn't him hiding his celebrity and his career, this was a child, and she understood the irreparable damage staying silent had inflicted on him.

She wished she didn't, but she did.

Paisley got to her feet and followed him. She thought she should apologize again but remembered how he'd kept on apologizing and it hadn't helped her. He was so rigid as he moved with none of his usual grace. She had no idea what to say. But as he got his coat out of the closet and stood there, putting it on, she knew she had to say something.

"I know that this is unforgivable and it would be easy for me to blame it on my past and the actions of my father. But the truth is, you aren't him and you've never lied to me about the important stuff. Even when you were Jack, you were still Sean. These last few weeks have shown me that."

He just stared at her, clenching his jaw, not saying a word, and she almost stopped herself. But this was her last chance to talk to him. They weren't going to run into each other at the coffee shop or the grocery store. When he walked out that door, he was going back to his world of celebrity and bodyguards.

"I was scared as much about my ability to raise this child as I was about trusting you to be the partner I needed. I watched my mom struggle with loving the wrong man and doing her best to raise us. And I know she did what she could but she failed us. And I don't hold that against her. I just wanted to make sure I was making the best choice for the child and our future and in that I failed."

He nodded stiffly. "I get all of that. A child scares the shit out of me, I'm not going to pretend it doesn't. My only parent was a nightmare and she didn't do it because she loved a broken partner, she did it because she was selfish and loved the limelight."

"You're not your mom," she said. "I never thought you wouldn't be a good father. I just didn't know who you really were. And now that I do… I wish I hadn't hesitated."

"Me too," he said, the words cold and hard.

There was nothing left to say. No more words she could use to help him understand and there were no words to heal this. *If they loved each other. If they trusted each other. If they believed…* But both of them were too weary for that.

"I guess this is goodbye then."

Goodbye. It had a feeling of finality and something made him hesitate. But the truth was with Paisley he had started to envision a different life and in that one moment, it was gone. There was no dream life waiting for him. It was all smoke and mirrors, as he should have known having worked in movies for as long as he could remember.

He caught a glimpse of himself in her hall mirror and realized that he looked tough and almost scary. Was this what she saw? Was that image part of why she'd held back? He knew that he couldn't ease the anger that was holding him rigid at this moment. It was all that was keeping him from losing it.

It would be easy to fool himself by saying he'd been swept up in the magic of the season, but the truth was he'd wanted to be swept into her world. He had felt like he'd found a place where he belonged. Paisley had started to feel like the kind of home he'd never had and hadn't realized he'd wanted.

"Yeah, I think so."

She nodded and blinked a few times. He suspected she was trying not to cry and he was dragging this out. He should just walk out the door but he still cared for her. Emotions didn't shut off just because he'd been hurt by her silence.

He cursed under his breath and pulled her into his arms, hugging her close to him as he remembered the high of the evening. The ring in his pocket that he'd tucked there, hoping that this was something that his gut seemed to know it wasn't.

"Goodbye, Paisley. It's been a ride," he said, kissing her temple and then pulling back because if he didn't he'd stay, even knowing how little she trusted him. She looked up at him with those large blue-gray eyes of hers swimming in tears and he felt a stab right in his heart. He'd never wanted to hurt her but he couldn't stay when she didn't believe in him.

If only the world's press could see this weakness, they'd have a hearty laugh at the strong, seemingly invincible playboy being brought to his knees by a woman. He'd always seemed so unscathed by the ending of his relationships and maybe because they'd been superficial he had been. But there had never been anything like that with Paisley.

Sean saw so many emotions in her eyes and turned before he gave in to the weakness inside of him and did something he'd end up regretting. So he opened her door and walked into the hall, closing the door firmly behind him. He leaned against it for a moment, felt the wreath brush against the back of his head and turned to look at the family that he'd found in Chicago. That wreath made him want to punch something. He wanted that to have been his new life, but the truth was just what his mom had said all those years ago.

People liked him better when he was playing at being someone else.

Except he'd never really been playing someone else, he realized suddenly. Those parts had always been the real Sean but just in a different skin. It was safer to be "real" when he was playing a role because the vulnerability couldn't hurt him. Not like this had.

He shook off his doubts and fears and walked down the hall to the stairs, and once he stepped outside, he noticed it was snowing and bitterly cold. The driver was still at the curb and started to get out of the car as Sean approached, but he waved at him to stay inside and opened the back door for himself.

"Take me home."

"Yes, sir."

Fifteen

Two days until Christmas, five days since she'd told Sean about the baby, and she was in the mall, walking around looking for…well, she wasn't sure what. *Something.* She stopped under the big tree that was in the center of the mall and just looked up at it.

"Knew I'd find you here and not just because of our friend-finder app," Olive said, slipping her arm around her. "Every time you leave the office you come here."

"How'd you know?" she asked. Olive was right. Every day since Monday, when she'd come back to work, she'd found herself down here. Looking for some kind of sign in the people around her or in the shops. Something that would trigger a good idea of what she could say or gift to Sean to make him see she knew she should have trusted him sooner.

"I asked Lyle to follow you," Delaney said, coming up on her other side. "We know you are sad."

"I'm not sad, not really. Maybe I am. It's just I can't figure out how to fix this. I mean, when Dad took Mrs. B's savings and her house to pay for my college, it was easy to find the solution." Giving back Mrs. B's home, even though it wasn't the one she'd lost, was something that was doable. But how could she win back trust that she'd shattered?

"You don't fix this," Delaney said. "You screwed up and you owned it. It's up to him to find his way back."

"Except he won't," she lamented. "I saw his face. I mean in that moment when I told him and saw what it did to him, I realized how much I loved him."

"Did you tell him that?" Olive asked.

"No, do you think it would have helped? He was pissed," she said, remembering the anger, but also the way he'd stepped away from her and brought it under control.

Olive shrugged. "When I found out that Dante had been the boy I humiliated in college, I was furious at him for keeping our past a secret. But once I calmed down, my love for him made me realize that it was both of our responsibilities to each other to forgive and move on."

"It was the same with me and Nolan," Delaney said. "He thought I'd played him and that made me mad because for the first time I wasn't trying to be anyone but me. It hurt that he saw in me what everyone else did. But once I had time to think about it…well, a life without him and Daisey was the last thing I wanted."

She put her arms around both of her friends. "Thanks, but you were both the one hurt and this time… I did this."

"But he started it, sort of. Like I did with Dante. If I hadn't been such a mean girl in college, I wouldn't have created something that he had to hide," Olive admitted. "Seems to me if Sean had been honest, then maybe you would have been too."

"Maybe. Truthfully, if I'd known he was Sean O'Neill I would never have flirted with him."

"Silly goose, you would too. There is something damn hot between the two of you," Delaney said.

"How do I win him back?"

"Big gesture?" Olive suggested.

"I don't think a big gesture will work for Sean. He's so careful about who he lets see the real man," she said.

"So do something big in front of the people who matter to him and to you," Olive said.

Something big. But what? She had hurt him by not trusting him, which meant she had to be vulnerable to him in a big way. And Olive was right…it needed to be in front of the people who mattered to them. The circle was small.

"I think he misses you," Delaney said.

"Why do you say that?"

"He's still in town," her friend said. "Nolan mentioned that he's seen Sean at the gym every day this week."

"I didn't know that." She'd have thought he would have gone back to LA, but she knew he had no one out there except his assistant, who was getting engaged.

"Dante invited him to the Feast of the Seven Fishes at his folks' house on Christmas Eve," Olive said. "You could do something there."

Like what? But that meant she had a target to try and figure it out.

"Honestly just talking to him would be good. What did he do to get back into your good graces?" Olive asked.

"He kept texting and when I didn't respond he had the studio hire us," she said. "He just didn't stop reaching out to me."

As she said it, she realized she hadn't done that. She'd gone radio silent, as was her way. Probably just confirming to him that he'd been right to walk away. Paisley thought about the moment she started to fall in love with Sean and knew it was that day at Mrs. B's. She knew then what she had to do. It was going to take this entire family that she'd built for herself.

Her sisters of the heart, Olive and Delaney, and their men, the ladies of Mrs. B's building and a sincere apology and baring her soul. She had been afraid to say that she loved him because the last time she'd let herself love she'd been hurt. And to be fair she hadn't let herself.

Love was just something that happened. She'd told Sean that her mom had loved the wrong man and it had broken their family, yet she'd never told him that his love could fix her and help make them a family.

"I've got it. I think I'm going to have a get-together tonight. Can you guys make it?"

"Of course," they both said at the same time.

"Good. Now I've got some shopping, planning and calls to make."

"You make the calls, I'll do the shopping," Delaney offered. "And Olive can do the planning. What do you have in mind?"

They sat down in the mall coffee shop and she outlined her plan. When she was finished, she felt like this was her best shot at getting Sean back and convincing him that they were meant to be.

Coffee with Dante had been nice and it had made Sean realize how despite everything, he'd made good friends here. He noticed Nolan at his gym and they talked as well. For the first time in his life he had friends who weren't in the business and didn't need him to help move their career forward.

Dante had invited him to something called the Feast of the Seven Fishes on Christmas Eve and even though he knew that Paisley was going to be there and that she hadn't called or texted since the night they broke up, he was going to go. His child was going to be a part of this friend network of hers and he needed to be as well.

Bert and his fiancée Christa had arrived and were settling into the guest house.

He'd done a lot of thinking about being a father. A parent. The word was as foreign to him as love was. He knew that this wasn't going to be an easy path. He'd researched roles before and had really gotten into the characters, understood their way of thinking, and he knew that fatherhood wouldn't be like any role he'd taken on before. But he also knew that he could do it.

First up, he'd decided he was going to buy a house here in Chicago. He knew that Paisley wasn't going to move to LA and he wanted to be close to the baby. When would they know if it was a boy or a girl?

He still had so much to learn.

Sean tried to keep from checking his phone because it made him feel like a chump, but he missed her. He was waiting for her to reach out to him, to tell him she was sorry again…yeah, he wanted to hear it one more time. His anger had burned out after the weekend, but pride wouldn't let him be the first to text.

Which was stupid and the reason why he was probably going to have to be fake-happy around Paisley and his child for the rest of his life. He didn't want to be the weaker one. He'd never been that in his life and didn't think he could start now.

Hell.

The buzzer for the gate rang and he opened the app to see who it was, hoping it was Paisley. But instead, there was a delivery guy.

He buzzed him in.

When he opened the front door, the guy handed him a box. "I love all your movies."

"Thanks."

"Can I get a photo? I know you probably get this all the time," he said.

"Sure, I don't mind. If you didn't watch my films, I wouldn't have a career," he said, smiling as the guy took a selfie with him.

"Thanks. Merry Christmas."

"You too."

The guy left and he realized that he hadn't felt Christmassy at all since he'd left Paisley's apartment. He doubted he would again. Sean had never expected anything special during the holidays. He'd done his best to just take them as they came but this year… it had been different. He remembered the trees and baking cookies and it hurt.

He opened the box and was surprised to see it was from Cass and the studio.

Sean and Paisley,
You left without your swag bags and your photo. It's such a cute one I knew you'd want it.
Happy holidays,
Cass

He set aside the swag bags, which he knew would be filled with luxury items that he probably already had or didn't need. Then he rummaged through the box until he found the photo frame at the bottom. It was a *Christmas Magic*-themed one and he felt like he'd been punched in the gut as he looked down at them.

He was holding her close and they were smiling at each other. His heart started to race. That was the moment when he'd had it all. He loved her; she was looking up at him like she loved him too.

And…

What? he asked himself. He hadn't stopped loving her because she'd withheld the truth about the baby. He still loved her, and seeing her face right now, he realized she might love him too. Had he misjudged the situation?

Could he forgive her for waiting so long to tell him she was pregnant?

When he put it like that, it felt somehow smaller than it was to him. She'd hurt him by not blindly trusting in him and in the love that he'd never spoken to her. How could he expect her to trust him when he didn't trust himself?

Sean reached for his phone. He'd send a text and see if she responded. He had her gift from the studio so that would be his ice-breaker.

He'd play it cool. But as he glanced down at the picture, he knew he couldn't fake being happy around her in the future if she wasn't with him. It was going to take him a long time to get over her. And he realized he didn't want to get over her.

He wanted to get her back.

He texted her. Hey, the studio sent some stuff for you to my place. Want to get together so I can give it to you?

Dancing dots. Then they disappeared. Crap. Then the dots were back after five minutes.

Paisley responded: Sure.

That was a long time for her to type one word.

How's tonight?

Actually I have an event at the office at 6 tonight. Can you stop by?

An event. Maybe she didn't want to be alone with him. Who cared? She'd said yes and he was going to make this most of this opening.

Great. See you then.

He put down his phone and went upstairs to shave, since he'd hadn't since he'd left her place. He took his time getting ready, making sure he looked every inch the Hollywood star that he was. He knew looks weren't going to sway her but he wanted to walk into her event as Sean O'Neill with all his confidence and swagger.

* * *

Paisley was nervous as she waited for Sean to appear. With the help of her friends she'd turned the conference room into a Christmas wonderland. A path wove under lighted arches and through Christmas trees. She'd decorated each of the trees with photos and mementos from their time together.

The first tree had a photo she'd snapped of him that first day at the coffee shop and had sent to Olive and Delaney with both the fire- and heart-eyes emojis. She had also picked up a logoed cup from the coffee shop that had his order written on it and a napkin where he'd written down his number for her because she had left her phone at the office that day.

Each tree moved further into their relationship with the snowy white one changing from the beginning of it until she'd found out that Jack was really Sean O'Neill. She hoped he'd see how deeply she'd fallen in love with him.

She got a message on her phone from the night security guard that he was here and she okayed him to come up. All of their friends including his assistant and fiancée were waiting at the end of the tree path and she sort of had a speech she wanted to say to him. But she wanted to show him everything that was in her heart while they were alone.

She heard the elevator car open and stepped out into the hallway, catching her breath when she saw him. Sean looked like he'd stepped off the cover of *GQ*'s sexy man edition. He was wearing a black suit that was cut to accentuate his broad shoulders, a white shirt and a red tie. His hair had been styled and he was freshly shaven. He raised both eyebrows at her when he saw her.

She wore the dress his designer friend had made for her. The dress, formfitting and made of red satin, hugged her curves and made her skin glow. It fell to the floor in a long pool of fabric and when she wore it she felt invincible. It seemed like the right dress to wear tonight. She wanted the night to end the way it should have after his premiere. But would her dream come true tonight? Could she earn his forgiveness, and together, could they celebrate their love for each other and their baby?

"I'm so glad you could come tonight," she said softly. "When you messaged me I was getting ready to reach out to you."

"I'm glad," he replied.

"I was trying to give you space to process everything…"

He nodded awkwardly. "Thanks."

Oh, this was so stiff and not going at all the way she had planned. He handed her a huge box.

"Wow. This is heavy."

"I know. Want me to put it in your office?" he asked, taking it back.

"No, you can leave it in here," she said as she opened the door to the conference room. "Just put it over there."

He set it on the floor where she'd gestured and

then straightened and looked at the forest of trees and winding path.

His eyes widened in surprise and he cocked his head to the side. "What is this?"

"This is for you. I wanted to show you what you meant to me. And that as much as I had been afraid to tell you about the baby, a part of me trusted you all along."

He stood next to the first tree, looking at the photos she'd sent of him to her friends and then moved along to the first time she'd invited him to have margaritas with Olive and Delaney. All of the time she'd spent with Jack…

"I was falling in love with Jack," she confessed as she led him to the white tree. She'd put a horse-drawn-carriage ornament on it and some cameras. "I was planning to tell you about the baby that night."

"But then you learned I wasn't the man you thought I was," he said quietly. "I wish things had gone better. I meant for that night to be all about the romance of what I could give you. To reassure you I was a man you'd want by your side."

She reached over impulsively and took his hand in hers, squeezing it as a tingle went up her arm. She started to pull back but he wove his fingers through hers and pulled her close to him.

"Paisley."

Just her name, but there was so much emotion in it that she felt her heart racing.

"Sean, I love you. I'm sorry I didn't tell you about the baby—"

"No, you couldn't have that night. I love you too," he said fiercely. "And I get it now. I understand that you needed some space to figure out who I really was."

She nodded and went up on tiptoe to kiss him. "I loved you all along and I just had to make sure that the man I loved was solid."

He kissed her back, long and deep, and when he lifted his head, she couldn't help the tears that ran down her face as he hugged her close and whispered in her ear. "I love you more than you can ever know. I may have looked to the world like a man who had everything, but until I had you and our baby, I didn't."

"Oh, Sean. I hope we will be good parents," she choked out. "I'm glad I'm not doing this alone."

"We will be the best parents we can be. I think we both have an idea of how *not* to be a parent," he said. "I'm glad you're not alone too."

He kissed her again and she felt his hands moving down her back—she knew where this was leading. She pulled back. "We're not alone at this party."

"We aren't?"

"Nope. We can finish that later," she said with a wink. "You haven't seen the rest of the trees."

"How many more are there?" he asked.

"Just one."

She led him around the tree to the next one. It was the one they'd decorated at her apartment. It was decorated with brightly colored twinkling lights. He saw the Boba Fett ornament and her Disney Princess. And their friends were all standing around it. "I wanted you to have our family here with you tonight. I know that my mistrust hurt you."

"But you still wanted to show me that I had a family with you?" he asked.

She nodded because she couldn't think of anything else to say. He hugged her again. "Thank you for giving me all this, Pais. You are the best present I've ever received at Christmas or any time."

"You are the same for me. I love you so very much and I think our child is lucky to have you as a father."

"I'm going to do my best to live up to that," he promised.

"I know you will."

Then he pulled her into his arms and dipped her low as he kissed her slow and deep. He had his world in his arms and he vowed to make sure he never let her slip out of them again.

Epilogue

One year later.

Paisley stepped out of the back of their house. They'd bought a home in the same neighborhood as Nolan, Delaney and Daisey. Olive and Dante had done the same as well. The three couples had grown closer and Sean was looking forward to seeing them all tomorrow night. Olive was six months pregnant with her first child and Nolan was trying to convince Delaney to have one too, according to Paisley.

Sean caught his breath as he always did when he saw her, her pretty blue-gray eyes lighting up as she noticed him. She smiled at him as she walked closer to him. Paisley had their son, whom they'd named

Jack, in her arms. She noticed the horse-drawn coach behind him and started laughing.

"When you said dress warmly, I wasn't sure what you had in mind. Now it makes sense," she said as she walked toward him. When she got closer, he reached out and took Jack from her, nestling his son close to his chest and kissing him on the forehead. The three-month-old drooled and did his sort of smile. He was wrapped warmly in a snug one-piece thermal suit and had a beanie on his head. The carriage was just for show. They weren't going to for a ride in it. But he wanted to ask Paisley to marry him and the carriage was the only place that felt right.

"Is it too cold for a few minutes?" he asked, gesturing to the carriage. It was the middle of the afternoon and the weatherman had predicted snow, but right now it was just sort of cloudy and cold. He had a space heater tucked into the carriage to keep them warm once they got into it.

His heart was so full when he looked at Paisley and his son. For all his fears that he wouldn't be a good father, he'd found that fatherhood suited him. But he was pretty sure it was because he was sharing the parenting duties with Paisley. The both of them knew what bad parenting looked like and were determined not to repeat it.

"No, it should be fine. Jack is snug and so am I," she murmured. "You look good, all clean-shaven and hair grown back to normal. Still looking sexy as ever."

Sean was just back from six weeks of shooting in Europe and he'd missed them both so much. He had been waiting for the right moment to ask her to marry him. He knew nothing about marriage but he did know that he wanted Paisley to be his wife. He wanted them to have a lifelong claim on each other.

He laughed at her comment before he helped her into the carriage, handing her Jack before he climbed in after her. He put a thick woolen blanket over her lap and settled in next to her. The last time he'd been here with her, he'd been so sure that he could convince her to change her life and go back to the West Coast with him. He hadn't realized that the one who needed the change had been him.

He took a deep breath as he slid his arm around her shoulders and pulled her into the curve of his body. He felt a stir of desire, but pushed it aside for now. He had important things to do before he made love to her.

"A year ago, I thought that this carriage was going to be the start of something new between us. No more lies, no more pretending to be something I wasn't, and as I had expected everything changed."

She smiled and shook her head as she laughed ruefully. "It sure did."

"I don't regret it. I wish I'd been the one to tell you my true identity but I think our path even though it was rocky was the right one."

"Me too," she said softly. "We needed that to realize how strong the bond of love was between us and to get us a ready to be parents."

"I'm still not sure I'm ready," he admitted. "But I am sure of one thing. You."

"Me too," she said. Then smiled and he leaned over to kiss her.

"I missed you when I was gone." He had left three times over the last year to film projects and each time he wished she could have come with him. This time he'd taken steps to start setting up his own film company in Chicago, so he would be more in control of his projects and could stay closer to home.

"I missed you too. I'm glad you made it home for December and all of our Christmas plans."

"Me too. I think if we do the same thing as last year it becomes a tradition."

"Are you a traditional kind of man?" she asked.

"Turns out I am. And that leads me to the real reason why I have us sitting out here in this carriage."

He shifted off the bench to his knee in front of her and took the ring box from his pocket. "Paisley Campbell, will you marry me?"

She let out a soft gasp and her eyes glistened with tears. "Yes!"

Jack let out one of his happy gurgles and Sean put the platinum-set, marquis-cut diamond ring on Paisley's finger, getting back on the seat next to her. He pulled them both into his arms, cradling them close as a light snow started to fall. He'd found the role that he'd never realized he'd been born to play when he met and fell in love with her.

"You can't resist with the perfect Christmas moments, can you?" she asked.

"No, I can't. I want everything to be our version of perfect."

He carried her and their son inside the house and they played Christmas music and danced with Jack until he went down for his nap. And then he made love to his fiancée and knew that he'd found more than he'd expected. He'd found a Christmas magic he'd never imagined existed.

* * * * *

Don't miss a single story in
The Image Project trilogy

Billionaire Makeover
The Billionaire Plan
Billionaire Fake Out

COMING NEXT MONTH FROM

#2929 DESIGNS ON A RANCHER

Texas Cattleman's Club: The Wedding • by LaQuette

When big-city designer Keely Tucker is stranded with Jacob Chatman, the sexiest, most ambitious rancher in Texas, unbridled passion ignites. But will her own Hollywood career dreams be left in the rubble?

#2930 BREAKAWAY COWBOY

High Country Hawkes • by Barbara Dunlop

Rodeo cowboy Dallas Hawkes has an injured shoulder and a suspicious nature. Giving heartbroken Sierra Armstrong refuge at his ranch is a nonstarter. But the massage therapist's touch can help heal his damaged body. And open a world of burning desire in his lonely bed...

#2931 FRIENDS...WITH CONSEQUECES

Business and Babies • by Jules Bennett

The not-so-innocent night CEO Zane Westbrook spent with his brother's best friend, Nora Monroe, was supposed to remain a secret. But their temporary fling turns permanent when she reveals she's expecting Zane's baby!

#2932 AFTER THE LIGHTS GO DOWN

by Donna Hill

It's lights, camera, *scandal* when competing morning-show news anchors Layne Davis and Paul Waverly set their sights on their next career goals. Especially as their ambitions and attraction collide on set...and seductive sparks explode behind closed doors!

#2933 ONE NIGHT WAGER

The Gilbert Curse • by Katherine Garbera

When feisty small-town Indy Belmont takes on bad boy celebrity chef Conrad Gilbert in a local cook-off, neither expects a red-hot attraction. Winning a weekend in his strong, sexy arms may be prize enough! But only if Indy can tame her headstrong beast...

#2934 BIG EASY SECRET

Bad Billionaires • by Kira Sinclair

Jameson Neally and Kinley Sullivan are two of the best computer hackers in the world. Cracking code is easy. But cracking the walls around their guarded hearts? Impossible! When the two team up on a steamy game of cat and mouse, will they catch their culprit...or each other?

Get 4 FREE REWARDS!

We'll send you 2 FREE Books plus 2 FREE Mystery Gifts.

FREE
Value Over
$20

Both the **Harlequin® Desire** and **Harlequin Presents®** series feature compelling novels filled with passion, sensuality and intriguing scandals.

YES! Please send me 2 FREE novels from the Harlequin Desire or Harlequin Presents series and my 2 FREE gifts (gifts are worth about $10 retail). After receiving them, if I don't wish to receive any more books, I can return the shipping statement marked "cancel." If I don't cancel, I will receive 6 brand-new Harlequin Presents Larger-Print books every month and be billed just $6.30 each in the U.S. or $6.49 each in Canada, a savings of at least 10% off the cover price, or 6 Harlequin Desire books every month and be billed just $5.05 each in the U.S. or $5.74 each in Canada, a savings of at least 12% off the cover price. It's quite a bargain! Shipping and handling is just 50¢ per book in the U.S. and $1.25 per book in Canada.* I understand that accepting the 2 free books and gifts places me under no obligation to buy anything. I can always return a shipment and cancel at any time by calling the number below. The free books and gifts are mine to keep no matter what I decide.

Choose one: ☐ **Harlequin Desire**
(225/326 HDN GRJ7)

☐ **Harlequin Presents Larger-Print**
(176/376 HDN GRJ7)

Name (please print)

Address   Apt. #

City   State/Province   Zip/Postal Code

Email: Please check this box ☐ if you would like to receive newsletters and promotional emails from Harlequin Enterprises ULC and its affiliates. You can unsubscribe anytime.

Mail to the **Harlequin Reader Service:**
IN U.S.A.: P.O. Box 1341, Buffalo, NY 14240-8531
IN CANADA: P.O. Box 603, Fort Erie, Ontario L2A 5X3

Want to try 2 free books from another series! Call 1-800-873-8635 or visit www.ReaderService.com.

*Terms and prices subject to change without notice. Prices do not include sales taxes, which will be charged (if applicable) based on your state or country of residence. Canadian residents will be charged applicable taxes. Offer not valid in Quebec. This offer is limited to one order per household. Books received may not be as shown. Not valid for current subscribers to the Harlequin Presents or Harlequin Desire series. All orders subject to approval. Credit or debit balances in a customer's account(s) may be offset by any other outstanding balance owed by or to the customer. Please allow 4 to 6 weeks for delivery. Offer available while quantities last.

Your Privacy—Your information is being collected by Harlequin Enterprises ULC, operating as Harlequin Reader Service. For a complete summary of the information we collect, how we use this information and to whom it is disclosed, please visit our privacy notice located at corporate.harlequin.com/privacy-notice. From time to time we may also exchange your personal information with reputable third parties. If you wish to opt out of this sharing of your personal information, please visit readerservice.com/consumerschoice or call 1-800-873-8635. **Notice to California Residents**—Under California law, you have specific rights to control and access your data. For more information on these rights and how to exercise them, visit corporate.harlequin.com/california-privacy.

HDHP22R3

HARLEQUIN
PLUS

Announcing a **BRAND-NEW** multimedia subscription service for romance fans like you!

Read, Watch and Play.

Experience the easiest way to get the romance content you crave.

Start your **FREE 7 DAY TRIAL** at
<u>www.harlequinplus.com/freetrial</u>.